VILLAINOUS HEARTS:

ACADEMY FOR VILLAINS BOOK 1

SCARLETT SNOW

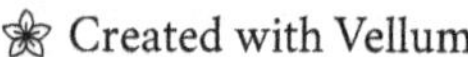 Created with Vellum

PROLOGUE

"The Furies have fallen, my lord. It won't be long before Cronos charges through the gates," Metheus declared, his tone laced with a concern that never before had been witnessed by another being; living or dead.

Hades cursed and turned away from the window, his black robes billowing behind him. The Grey Sisters had long foreseen that this night would come. Hades was able to find a way out, and while it had been a last resort, it was still a chance. He would take any chance necessary if it meant he could save Persephone from his father's wrath.

"What do you wish me to do now, my lord?" Metheus glanced out the window to where the Gates of Erebus were being destroyed in the near distance.

Hades faced his old friend and clapped him on the shoulder. "Flee while you still can."

The seer's white eyebrows lifted in alarm and defiance. "I cannot leave you here."

"Take my chariot and flee. There is nothing more to be done here. You have served me well, my old friend. Make haste before it is too late."

He turned before Metheus could protest and entered his chamber. Persephone, draped in a sheer pink gown that flowed at her feet, paced on the balcony. The ground shook as Cronos finally broke through the gates.

"It is time," Hades softly informed her.

Persephone paused in her tracks and looked up at him. "But…" Her hand fell to her swollen stomach. "Our children."

Hades took her hand in his and lifted her gaze with his other. "They will one day be reborn in the next life with us."

Tears slipped from her lashes. "Yes. We must do this for our future and for our children. There is no other way."

Indeed, there was not. This was the only way they could be together without Cronos and his followers trying to kill Hades now that he had escaped Tartarus. The Titan was determined to kill his firstborn one way or another, and none of the other gods dared help because they were too occupied with their own realms.

"I am frightened, my love," Persephone whispered, closing her eyes.

"Do not fear the darkness that is to come." Hades reached into his robe and withdrew two crystal vials. "For I will be there to guide the way through." He opened one of the vials and ran the lid along Persephone's bowed lips. Slowly, she opened, and he reached for the back of her neck, then poured the liquid onto her tongue. Persephone swallowed the contents while tears streamed down her cheeks. "I will love you for eternity, my ílios, in this life, and the thousands after it."

Persephone opened her eyes and took the second vial from him. "And I love you, my astéri, until the last breath of our last life together." She poured the liquid into his mouth. "Nothing in all the realms will keep us apart. Not Cronos. Not Gaia. No one, no thing." She pressed her lips to his, her heart clenching with despair.

Hades wrapped his arms around her waist and held her close. "Do not forget me."

"Never, my love."

And then they leapt, falling to their deaths.

"Why do villains get punished for having fun?" I sit down on the beach next to my sister and glance up at the blinding sunlight. "One tiny hiccup and now we're stuck at the Academy for Villains for three whole months. It's so unfair."

"You turned a guy's dick into stone and snapped it like a glow stick." Murie side-eyes me with an amused grin sliding over her lips. "What did you think would happen?"

I give a casual shrug. "He touched my butt, so I broke his dick. No touchy, no hurty." Tossing my long pink hair over my shoulders, I follow her gaze. The sun has nearly touched the horizon. That means the ship will be here soon, and my stomach clenches at the thought. "Anyway, it was my hair that turned him into stone, not me."

She snorts under her breath. "Blame it on your half Gorgon side like you always do."

"Hey, it's a legit excuse. I'm cursed!"

Murie drapes her arm over my shoulders, her feet buried in the water lapping at the shore. "And I'm cursed too, Zara. This academy is the only place for people like us."

"Those who are fucked up and not all there in the head?"

She laughs and playfully shoves my shoulder. "Bad-ass women who don't need a knight in shining armour to save them."

"I'd probably just break his dick off anyway," I grumble. "Maybe by accident this time. Maybe. Unless he turns out to be another jerk, in which case I will happily turn his dick into stone and snap it like a glow stick." I stand and brush the sand off my green plaid skirt. "Unfortunately, I doubt the academy will let us use magic."

Murie pauses, brushing her silver hair behind her pointed ears. "Probably not but it's worth a try."

"Have I taught you nothing?"

Our mother's voice carries on the ocean breeze. We turn to see her emerging from the sea; the waves lapping at her waist. Her purple tentacles vanish and a long, flowing gown of dark seaweed covers her now human body. Her silver hair and lilac complexion are the same as Murie's.

My pale skin, pink eyes and hair are the complete opposite. I'm also part Gorgon and can't breathe underwater. It doesn't take a genius to see that I'm the adopted one.

"Rules are meant to be broken." My mother dips her

toes into the white sand, a smile dancing over her lips. "Be proud of who you are and show no fear."

I grin at her. "Fear? I laugh in the face of fear."

As if on cue, the sand beneath my boots trembles. The sun has touched the horizon at long last and it stains the clouds with streaks of crimson and gold. In the far distance, a shadow eclipses the setting sun. I shield my gaze from the blinding rays and watch as a monstrous dragon-shaped ship with black sails glides towards us. It should take some time for the ship to reach the shore, but it arrives only minutes later.

My heart picks up its pace as I watch the anchor plunge into the sea. A gangway is dropped down, but at first, nobody disembarks. The dragon wings slowly curl inward and then I see it, the cloud of dark energy seeping down the ramp. A hooded man materialises from the smoke, the shadows licking around his tall frame.

"Captain Nemo." He inclines his head curtly and then looks between me and Murie. His eyes cut into us like sharpened sea glass, the same ocean-blue as the turban wrapped around his head. "Are you the Eyre sisters?"

"Depends. You here to take us to our doom?" I ask, crossing my arms. "Also, Nemo? As in the fish?"

Murie nudges me with her elbow. "Yes, we are the Eyre sisters."

Rolling my eyes, I give the ship an assessing once over. The deck looks empty from where I'm standing. Surely, we're not the first ones to get picked up? As I push up onto my tiptoes, the captain snaps his fingers, and something sharp pricks me on the side of the neck. It's like a mosquito bite, only sharper.

"What's that for?" I rub where he struck, my irritated pulse fluttering under my fingers.

"A precaution."

"For what?"

He doesn't answer me. After doing the same to Murie, he says, "Say your farewells. It is time to set sail."

I salute him. "Aye aye, Cap'n."

Nemo pivots on his heel and makes his way back to the ship. No sense of humour, huh? Figures.

"Remember what I said, darlings." Mother turns us around and cups the side of our faces. "Be proud and show no fear."

The concern in her eyes is mirrored within my own, despite my bravado. My biggest coping mechanism in life has always been making light of serious situations. The twisted sense of humour I've adopted over the years has got me through some of my darkest moments. But I know, and my family knows, that deep down I'm just as worried as they are.

"Did I ever tell you why I called you Zara Primrose?"

Her question takes me off guard. My mother rarely ever talks about the day she found me. All I know is that my birth parents left me in a basket outside a stone temple and my mother heard my cries from under the sea. She swooped me into her arms and the rest was history.

"You had this around your neck when I found you."

My mother reaches into her pocket and withdraws a stone primrose hanging on a long silver chain. "I couldn't touch it without the pendant burning me. You used to wear it every day until you were about four, then you lost it while out swimming with Muriel."

"I remember that," my sister says.

"I don't."

My mother nods thoughtfully. "You cried for months. I searched everywhere for it but assumed it was lost. Then it showed up at the market in Atlantis the same day you turned that hideous young man into stone."

My eyes widen in surprise, and I take the pendant from her. "It's beautiful."

"And it's yours. It's enchanted, too, so you'll be able to use it to contact me. All you need to do is sit the primrose in water and say my name three times."

Tears prick my eyes as I drape the chain over my neck, tucking the pendant under my shirt.

"I just want you both to be safe," Mother whispers, taking our hands. "By all means, break the rules whenever necessary, but pick those battles. And also don't forget your old mama. Murie, have you got your pendant, too?"

"Yes." Murie taps her pocket and then hugs her. "Try not to worry, Mum. Zee and I will have each other's backs, right?"

"Right," I say, joining in on the embrace

The three of us stay like that for a long while. When the ship sounds its horn, we know it's time and reluctantly let go before heading over to the ship. I try not to look back. It'll just make boarding the ship that much harder.

A nearly invisible veil has been wrapped around the ship. Humans wouldn't be able to see it thanks to the concealment spell. As soon as we step onto the ramp, the spell lifts, and crew members buzz around the deck. Some other students have already been picked up, but I'm drawn to one in particular. Maybe it's because he's grinning like he's just won the cruise of a fucking lifetime.

He's tall and pale with ebony hair that brushes his shoulders. His emerald tunic has gold embroidery, and his black cloak whips around him as he rushes up the stairs to grab hold of the wheel. The force field protecting the wheel sends him spiraling onto his back, much to the delight of the captain and his crew.

I wince as he lands on the deck with a loud slap and splutters for breath.

"Let that be a lesson to any fool wanting to take over my ship," Captain Nemo announces, pulling out a scroll and quill, gesturing to the boy. "Loki of Asgard. What sin has brought you to the Academy for Villains?"

Loki rises to his feet and brushes the dust off his clothes. "What do you think, old man?"

"I see. So you tried, yet again, to take over Asgard but failed?"

The boy's face purples with anguish. "Yes," he grits out.

Captain Nemo tuts and shakes his head, scribbling something down on the scroll. "Dear, oh dear. Perhaps next time you will be successful and not get caught."

He turns to my sister. "Muriel Eyre. What is your sin?"

Murie hesitates and looks at me for support. I open my mouth to speak on her behalf, but the captain cuts me off.

"She has a tongue and can answer for herself."

After a strained moment, my sister takes a deep breath. "I let a pirate drown at sea. I could've saved him, but I… I choose to swim away."

"She was also just a kid herself, and the pirate killed our dad before trying to poach her," I defend, narrowing my eyes on the captain. My hair bristles like a wave of static electricity as the snakes threaten to take over. "She shouldn't even be here!"

He just scores something off, not bothering to look up from his scroll. "And you, Zara-Primrose. What sin did you commit?"

All eyes turn to me, including Loki.

Right. Now it's my turn to tell the truth.

Only, I'm not embarrassed to say it. I embrace what I did to that little pervert.

"I turned a man's junk into stone, then I broke it off and wore it as a necklace. That's what he gets for pissing off a gorgon."

To my surprise, a lot of the crew members and students just laugh. Do they think it's a joke? Honey, I still have that stone dick in my bedroom back home. It's sitting on my vanity like a prized fucking trophy. These men would be wise not to get on my bad side. I'm not above adding to my collection. My mother always said I like to hoard things.

Captain Nemo interrogates the remaining students while the crew propels the ship into motion. I stand beside Murie, watching the waves crash against the surface. The dragon wings attached to the side stretch out, then start to move, lifting us up into the clouds. Okay. So the boat can fly. Thank goodness I'm not super afraid of heights or anything, or that would be a real inconvenience right about now.

Murie links her arm with mine. "This is it, Zee. No turning back."

We couldn't even if we wanted to, I almost say, but I don't want to worry her even more. I rest my head on her shoulder and watch the sea growing smaller beneath us. We might not have a choice when it comes to going to the Academy for Villains, but I hope, for the sake of the students and teachers there, they are ready to meet the Eyre sisters.

We're villains now.

And I will not hold back anymore.

*I*f someone told me before setting off that the Academy for Villains was a castle sitting on top of a floating island, I would've laughed and asked to make mine a double shot. But that's exactly what the academy is. The boat drifts through the clouds and lands seamlessly on the lake surrounding the castle on the centre of the island.

First, the anchor is dropped, then the gangway, and one by one everyone disembarks. There's already a ship docked with students gathered beside the lake. Damn, the captain of that ship is all tattooed and rugged. I'd swap him for the fish cap'n any day of the week.

No. Enough, Zara. You are *not* here to date.

With that bitter reminder, I follow Murie to where everyone's gathering around a man in long ebony robes. Everything from his cloak to his suit and cane is black, but the mask covering half of his face is pure white. We stop at the front of the crowd and I can see a scar poking out from the edge of his mask. Whatever he's hiding can't be pretty.

"Good-evening… students."

The lengthy pause makes my heart jump. He might as well have just called us prisoners.

"For those who have not attended here before, I'm Eryc Knightford, the headmaster of the Academy for Villains. I am delighted to meet you all." His face and tone say otherwise. "I see we have some familiar faces that have decided to join us for another term. Welcome back." Knightford's dark eyes land on Loki for a moment, then return to scanning the other students. When they find me, he seems to pale a little around the gills. He clears his throat and quickly looks away. "Let me make one thing clear: I do not tolerate rule-breaking on my island. You have each been assigned your terms prior to arriving. Some of you are here for only three months while others are here for much longer."

"Just like a prison," someone mutters in the back of the crowd.

Knightford's expression doesn't even falter. "At the end of your final term, the board of directors and I will decide if you have atoned for your sin and then you will be returned to your families."

"And what happens if you decide we haven't atoned?" I press him, crossing my arms.

His eyes flash my way again. For an awkwardly long moment, he just stares at me. "You will be sent to the underworld until Lucifer decides to release your soul." Clearing his throat, he adds almost derisively, "Think of this academy as a second chance. Follow my rules, pass your tests with flying colors, and your time here will be swift and painless."

"Yup," I whisper to Murie. "This is totally a prison."

She sniggers but coughs into her hand when Knightford glares at her.

"You have each been assigned to a house," the headmaster resumes. "There are seven in total and allocations have been decided upon based on which sin brought you here. I will now hand you over to our matron, Miss Torrigan."

A young woman steps forward. When the sun hits her auburn hair, each strand shimmers like iridescent scales. Something tells me she's a mermaid. I listen to her call out everyone's name and assign their houses. I'm not surprised when Murie and I are given Wrath.

"We're going inside," Murie says, linking my arm with hers. Her teeth are chattering, which I know is a nervous habit of hers. "Confession, I'm freaking out."

"Me too, but don't worry. We're in this together."

She nods and pats my hand shakily. I swallow down my own nerves and follow everyone onto the bridge. We barely step on it when a hand clamps on my shoulder and tugs me away from Murie. The same hand pulls me into a tight embrace, my face pressed against a muscular chest, and my senses fill with a heady cologne.

"I thought I'd never see you again!"

See me again? I shove my fists into his chest and push him back. He lets go reluctantly and I take a good, hard look at him. It's evident immediately that I have never seen this boy before. I'd remember his fiery-blue hair and amber eyes. His irises are vertical, almost like a dragon, but dragons don't have such flawless complexions. This boy's pale skin is absent of any scales, though there's an apparent glow about him, like the coronas of the moon. He's hot—that much is clear—but he's also mistaking me for someone else.

"You don't remember me?" He searches my eyes with a pained look drifting over his face. "My love..."

"Okay, big guy. I'm gonna stop you riiiight there." I step away from him, my body tensing in anger. Hot or not, I'm getting some weird vibes from him. "I have no idea who or what the fuck you are."

"Who's this?" Murie stops at my side and eyes the boy just as skeptically.

I shrug at her. "Hell if I know. I think he's gunning for a black eye because he keeps calling me his love."

The boy's eyebrows knit together. "It's me... It's Hades!"

I eye him curiously. "Neat name but I still don't know who you are."

"I've waited many years for you, my lo—"

"Don't call me that," I warn, seconds away from losing my shit.

"This can't be right. We're meant to be together!" Hades steps forward and grabs my arm.

For what feels like an eternity, I just stare at his hand gripping me like a vise. My heart rate spikes and my blood runs cold in my veins, pounding furiously in my ears. Before I can stop it, my power takes over and pink fire explodes from my body like a shield, knocking Hades off the bridge and into the water. I march over to the side and point at him, my serpent hair hissing in warning.

"Stay the hell away from me you sexy sonovabitch psychopath!"

Hades splutters water from his mouth and grasps the edge of the pier. Lifting my hand to hex him, Murie pulls me back and drags me across the bridge to the castle. My hands are shaking and my pulse thrashes in my ears when we reach the other side. Gods, I want to kill him!

"Who even is that psycho?" I glance at Murie, hoping she can shed light on the asshole that is Hades because I sure as hell don't remember him.

"That *psycho* is our Defense teacher's son," Loki quips as he walks past us, winking at me in particular. "Nice going there, snake girl. You sure know how to put on a good show."

I glare at the back of his head. I'm tempted to let one of my snakes bite him on the ass just for calling me that. Murie's hand on my shoulder helps to remind me of where I am.

"Urgh," I grumble at her. "Villains get punished for having fun and the cute guys are always batshit crazy." I look up at the sky and shout from the top of my lungs: "If the gods could stop fucking with me now, that would be great!"

"Shhh, they can hear you," Murie hisses in a whisper.

She actually believes the Sea God can hear our every word.

"He's too busy riding waves and eating oysters to pay any attention," I tell her, my hair turning back to normal.

She laughs just as the shadow of the castle stretches over us. It's way bigger up close than I thought it would be. The doors are already open and we hurry through with everyone else. Seven people await our arrival in the conical vestibule. They stand in a straight line and they're all different species, from vampires and fae to centaurs and sea creatures. My eyes land on the boy standing at the end, the only one not in a school uniform. His black shirt is tucked a little sloppily into his jeans, his sleeves are rolled up to the elbow, and his red tie brings out his crimson eyes. He catches me staring at him and flashes a grin while dragging a hand through his wavy, jet-black hair. His fangs gleam in the light pouring down from the sconces on the walls.

Vampire. Of course.

I peel my gaze from him and focus on the boy breaking up the line. His silver cornrow hair stands out against his dark complexion and he has blue dots painted on his chiselled jaw and around his eyes. I'm not overly familiar with the markings, but something tells me they're to do with Atlantis. I bet Murie would know.

"Wrath new bloods," the boy shouts in a deep, husky voice. "I'm Kallias. Follow me."

Kallias turns on his heel and climbs the stairs without a backward glance. A group of students rush after him. As I prepare to follow in Murie's wake, the headmaster pulls me to the side.

"Miss Eyre, I would like a word with you in my office."

My heart sinks a little. I know it's about Hades.

"But my things—"

"I have already sent them to your room. Muriel will handle them, won't you?" He slides her a veiled glance, and my sister nods vigorously, her mouth agape. "Then it is settled. Come with me."

Casting Murie a longing glance, I have no choice but to follow Mr Knightford through the crowd of students. He leads me down a maze of corridors until we reach a gold staircase that spirals like a coiled dragon. I can see my scowl in the reflection of the banister. At the top, we enter an open-planned office with dark wooden furniture and bookshelves towering over a broad desk. Everything is clinically neat, from the polished floorboards to the three pencils aligned neatly on his desk beside a small stack of paperwork. I could use the desk as a mirror, it has been polished so much. Mr Knightford motions me to sit at the other side, and as I do so, I hear the door lock.

My pulse spikes and I crane my neck, watching as he walks over to his desk. He doesn't sit in his high-backed leather chair as I anticipate, choosing instead to gaze out the large, floor-to-ceiling window with his hands clasped behind his back. A deafening silence stretches between us and I grow desperate to break it. If I am to be punished, I'd rather he just got on with it.

"I'm sorry for lashing out earlier," I start, watching him turn on one heel.

The unmasked section of his face looks startled as

his gaze lands on me. He lifts a brow and widens his eyes, for a moment looking somewhat startled, and yet, the glimmer of emotion vanishes as quickly as it emerges. It's like he has pulled on another mask to hide behind. I bet he does that a lot. He doesn't strike me as the emotional kind.

"Yes, I must say your actions disappoint me." Settling into his seat, Mr Knightford straightens and splays his hands flat on the desk, his face now wiped clean of emotion. "I do not tolerate violence, Miss Eyre, especially toward a member of my faculty. However, am I right in thinking you were perhaps defending yourself?"

I nod, and he clicks his tongue.

"Then I will dismiss what transpired earlier. Frankly, I don't tolerate unsolicited physical contact either and I will be having words with Hades to get to the bottom of his actions. Rest assured, he will not step out of line again. If he does, you will report to me. Understood?"

I nod, telling him, "The boy claimed to know me, and yet I have no memory of him."

Mr Knightford nods thoughtfully. "I would suggest you steer clear of him. Hades is not the kind you want to be associated with."

My stomach clenches nervously. "What did he do to be sent here?"

"Hades single-handedly took down an entire Para-normal Crime Unit. He freed thousands of criminals for a cause he has yet to disclose. Hades will spend the rest of his days here until he confesses and it is my job to ensure that he does."

I blow out a whistle. "Whoa. So he's the real deal, huh? I mean, when it comes to villains."

Mr Knightford just stares at me.

"Cue laughter," I mumble.

He frowns. "I don't understand?"

"I said I'll be sure to steer clear of him, sir."

He nods and the long pause is extremely uncomfortable. I notice how tense his shoulders are and how much he's clenching his hands into fists, his knuckles blanched.

"Is that all, sir?"

"There is one more thing... I'm your father."

I gawk at him. So the headmaster of this academy is also crazy? Great. Just fan-fucking-tastic.

"Okaaaay then, sir. While it was good talking with ya, you should know that I'm not Luke Skywalker. I'm not a Jedi or Stormtrooper or whatever the hell happens in that thing. It's Murie's favourite, not mine. I've always preferred Lord of the Rings. If you'd told me that I must take the One Ring to Mordor then maybe I would understand, but—"

"Your mother left you outside the Forbidden Temple," he interjects, and every inch of his expression tells me that he truly believes what he's saying. "She was tricked by a sorcerer into believing the Temple of the Gods would heal you, that the gods would remove your curse. By the time I found out, you were already gone."

He stands from his chair; the movement making me

flinch, and walks around his desk to my side. Taking my hand into his, he stares intently into my eyes, and suddenly I notice how similar we are. Our eyes are the same, except for the color, and he has a dimple on his chin like I do. I'm still not entirely sure I believe him.

"For eighteen years, I have looked for you. I was beginning to wonder if perhaps you were lost forever, but the gods have smiled upon us this day and reunited a grieving father with his long-lost daughter. You're as much a part of me as my flesh and bones, and I don't ever want to lose you again."

Despite my best efforts, I blink the tears from my lashes and they roll onto our clasped hands. Mr Knightford moves his hand to retrieve a photograph from his inner coat pocket. He turns it around, and more tears fall.

It's me.

I must be only a few months old and I'm being carried in the arms of a young, beautiful woman. She's smiling at the camera and holding me up like I'm the best thing in all the realms. My hair is short and curly, not a single snake in sight. I always thought I was born with the curse. But this makes me wonder if it happened at a later time.

"This is my mum?" I take the photo from him, committing every detail to my memory. We have the same nose and lips and color of hair. She's also wearing a primrose necklace, but unlike mine, it's not made of stone. "What happened to her?"

Mr Knightford pushes off his desk and turns away. I follow him with my gaze over to the window, watching as he loses himself once again to contemplation.

"She died shortly after losing you. Your mother was never the same after it. She blamed herself for your curse and only wanted to help you, but when she came back to see if you had been cured, you were gone."

"Seceila took me," I whisper, looking back at the picture, my hand going to the necklace hidden under my shirt. "She heard me crying and took me with her. What was my mother's name?"

He turns, just a fraction. "Yvanna."

"Yvanna," I repeat the name slowly. "It's very beautiful."

"Your mother had a beautiful soul. I see her in you."

The compliment makes me blush and feel all warm inside. For all my life, I have thought that my biological parents abandoned me because they hated me. Now I'm told they only left me because they wanted to help me. To *cure* me. My head spins with so many questions. Was my curse really so terrifying that I was worth giving up?

"We have much to discuss," Mr Knightford says, walking back over and taking my hands in his. "For now, you must rest. You've had a long journey."

"But I have too many questions."

He smiles, the lines around his eyes crinkling. "As do I. We have the next three months to ask them, and the rest of our lives, if you'll let me be part of yours. I don't want to lose you again, Zara."

My chest tightens at the tears gathering into his

eyes. All I can do is hug him in reply. When I pull away, he folds my fingers around the photograph.

"Keep it. Your mother would want you to."

Words fail me. I can only nod as I slide the picture into my pocket and stand from the chair. The exhaustion pulling at my bones is overwhelming. I so desperately want to ask him all the things, but he's right. We have the rest of our lives to make up for lost time.

I leave his office and follow the signs for the dormitories. After Kallias shows me to my room, I find Murie draping her favorite blanket over the foot of her single bed. She rushes over when she sees me and grabs me by the shoulders.

"What's wrong? Did Hades annoy you again? I swear to Poseidon, I will bitch slap him with all six of my tentacles."

"It wasn't Hades." I show her the photograph, my heart racing despite the smile curving my lips. "I just met my real dad. He's the headmaster."

CHAPTER THREE

"I can't believe it," Murie says for the one-hundredth time. "Mr Knightford is your dad."

"Tell me about it. First, I get attacked by a loco cutie, then the headmaster says he's my biological dad and it's not even..." I glance at my watch. "Six-thirty. Way too early for this shit. But that does remind me. Food?"

Murie stares at me like I've grown another head. "How can you think about food at a time like this?"

"How can I not? We haven't eaten in like two hours."

"Has it been that long already?" She grasps her stomach in mock horror.

"Come on. Let's see what food this prison—I mean, academy—has to offer."

I drag her by the hand out from our room. Much to my surprise, once we finally reach the canteen after only two wrong turns, the variety of food isn't half bad. We grab some burgers and look for a place to sit. My gaze lands on Hades who stands only five feet away from me, his knuckles blanched white as he holds his dinner tray. He takes one hard look at me before turning on his heel and marching off.

That guy is going to cause me trouble. I'm sure of it.

"Zee, over here," Murie says, nodding at the only vacant table in the cafeteria.

We set our trays down and dig into our food. It's the first chance I get to assess my fellow students and I'm amazed by how normal they all look. Sure, some of them are staring at me like I'm an unusual commodity, probably because I had a fight on my first day, but they look harmless enough.

Well, as harmless as any other young offender can look.

I lift my veggie burger and go to take a bite. That's when I notice the shadows in the corner of the hall. I can just make out a pair of legs, and a hand resting on the table. A crimson ring on his finger gleams in the light and so do the eyes hidden in the darkness.

"There's someone staring at us," I say to Murie, putting my burger down.

She looks around the hall, wiping the ketchup off her upper lip with her tongue. "Almost everyone's been staring at us after you knocked Hades on his ass." Her gaze lands on the shadows and she frowns. "Oh, him. I heard about him from Kal."

"Kal?" Now it's my turn to frown as I look at her. "Who's Kal?"

"Kallias, our year head. He helped carry your luggage up to our room and we saw the Shadow Boy on our way. I thought Kal was gonna slug him one." She lowers her voice and leans in, and I notice she's dropped ketchup onto her shirt. Typical Murie. "Apparently, everyone blames him for the death of a girl who died here last year."

"That's horrible. Did you catch his name?"

"Dracula."

"As in *the* Dracula? Prince of Darkness? Vlad the Impaler?" I glance at the boy, but he's no longer there.

"Not *the* Dracula. It's his son," Murie answers, swallowing the last of her burger. "Got sent here for trying to take over his father's castle in Transylvania."

"Actually, I'm afraid you are mistaken," a soft, velvety voice whispers, making me jump in my seat. "I was sent here for another reason entirely."

We turn to see Dracula standing behind us. My breath hitches as I realise he's the vampire I saw earlier —one of the Head Boys. A grin slides onto his lips and he runs a hand through his short wavy hair, flashing a series of black hoops hanging off his pointed ear. He's much taller than I expected and paler. His black coat slides around his knees, the intricate patterns are a vibrant blood-red, just like his eyes and the ring on his finger. There's now no doubt in my mind who this vampire is.

"I'll give you a hint," he says, winking at me. "Inimă mea."

"Is that Romanian?" I ask, loving his sexy accent.

He nods and wiggles his eyebrows at me. "The most romantic language in the world."

Murie snorts and shoves a handful of fries into her

mouth. He looks between us with an amused smirk on his face.

"Now let me guess why you two are here." He places his hands on the table in front of me and peers into my eyes. His glowing red ones search mine as though he's reading my thoughts. "Ah, I thought as much. You were sent here because you turned someone's wood into stone."

We stare blankly at him, though I struggle to keep the smile off my face.

Dracula huffs at his lack of applause. "Come on, admit it. That was hilarious."

"Ever heard of personal space?" I push back in my chair, my smile getting the better of me. "And it was hilarious. But you clearly heard me talking about it on the ship."

He holds up his hands with an even cheekier smirk. "Guilty as charged."

"Stalking your prey already." Loki sets his tray down with ours and glares at Dracula. "I've heard about what you do to the fresh meat around here." He holds two fingers to his lips, mimicking fangs.

Dracula's playfulness vanishes as he straightens off the table. A shadow drops over him like a veil of darkness. "It's soon to be Count Dracula to you."

"Do you mean *Cunt* Dracula?" Loki scoffs, his eyes narrowing into emerald shards. "Because that fits you more."

Murie and I gape at each other. While this exchange is entertaining, it seems like Loki is being a complete jerk to Dracula for no good reason. Then again, he was a jerk to me earlier. Maybe he's just a jerk.

"Funny," Dracula spits out. "I don't see you with a legitimate title, Loki of Assgard."

"It's *Asgard*, and you shouldn't be here after what you did!"

Loki snaps his fingers, and a gold scepter materialises into his hand. As quickly as the weapon appears, Dracula grabs the blade and pushes Loki back. His blood permeates the air as Loki pushes the blade as hard as he can, but Dracula doesn't so much as flinch when it cuts him.

"This is no way to act in front of ladies," he says in a deceptively calm voice. "And you're right. I am famished and your throat is looking rather tempting."

Just as his fangs extend, and he leans forward, a familiar voice bellows behind us.

"That is enough!" Knightford stands between them, his face twisted in anguish. "Retract your fangs and put your weapon down immediately!"

The entire cafeteria has come to a halt now, gathering around to witness the scene. I'm just glad it's not me they're ogling at this time. After a long, strained moment, Dracula's fangs disappear and Loki's scepter vanishes into thin air.

"Come with me," Knightford demands, and, casting me a glance, he marches the boys out of the cafeteria.

I have a feeling my list of troublemakers has just gone up by two. First Hades, and now Loki of Asgard and the Prince of Darkness. This really isn't how I expected my first day to go.

CHAPTER FOUR

"You go first," Murie whispers, nudging my arm.

"Nu-uh." I back away from the trapdoor and shake my head at her. "That looks like some serious entrance to Hell bullshit. You're older therefore I think *you* should go first."

The two of us stare at the trapdoor, except it's far too big to be that. A ladder clings to the edge where nothing but darkness lingers below. I can't see anything, but I can hear other students whispering and objects being moved around. Why does our first lesson need to be in a creepy dungeon?

"Maybe we came to the wrong place," I say, rummaging through my satchel for our class schedule. I pull it out and Murie walks around the door to peer over my shoulder at it:

Monday - Reparation One (Magical

*Arts) with Mrs Morgana in the
Oubliette
Tuesday - Reparation Two (Potions)
with Mrs Athame in the
Greenhouse
Wednesday - Reparation Three
(Magical Defense) with Mr Erebus
Thursday - Reparation Four (Theory)
with Mr Blackbird in the Main Hall*

"Nope." Murie sighs, tucking her hair behind her ears. "This is most definitely an Oubliette. But I don't know what Reparation One is really about."

"Allow me to explain, ladies." Loki slides between us, draping his arms over our shoulders. "Reparation is basically another word for doing the teachers' dirty work. Down there,"—he nods into the Oubliette—"is where we fix cursed objects as part of our punishment."

Despite the lurch my heart gives at our close proximity, I shrug him off and stuff my schedule back into my bag. What is it with the guys here and their lack of personal space? It's not that I hate physical contact. But I do dislike when people, especially men, think it's acceptable to touch others they barely know without their consent.

The last guy who did that got his dick turned into stone.

"What do you mean by cursed?" Murie asks, no doubt seeing the annoyance on my face. I've never been good at schooling my expressions. "It says here that

Rep One is also Magical Arts with... What was the name again, Zee?"

"Morgana."

"Right. Mrs Morgana. What kind of cursed things are we going to be fixing?"

Loki steps onto the ladder. "Usually it's ancient arti-facts. It's the best Rep class if you ask me. The rest are a total waste of time." He glances at the watch on his wrist and starts to climb down. For a long moment, Murie and I just stare into the darkness. "Sorry to disappoint you but I'm still alive," he calls out, and I release a breath I wasn't aware I was holding. "Are you coming down or what?"

"Of course we are!" I roll my shirt sleeves up and rotate my neck, flexing my arms as though I'm about to enter a fight. "Okay, Murie. I'm goin' in."

I step onto the ladder and slowly climb down. Murie follows me, and before I know it, the three of us are standing in a dimly lit passageway. Strange objects and old, tattered luggage line the walls. My breath streams out before me as I follow Loki with Murie close at my heels. Before we reach the open door at the end, Loki places a hand on my arm and I freeze to the spot. The usual smugness is gone from his face as he looks into my eyes.

"Can we talk alone for a moment?"

I look down at his hand on my arm. "If you let go of me, yes."

Murie enters the classroom but remains lingering by the door, still hesitant to leave me alone with a stranger. I love that she's so protective of me. We always have been with each other. I guess the irony is that it's our protectiveness that brought us here.

"I think we got off on the wrong foot," Loki says, removing his hand.

I arch my brows in mock surprise. "Really? Because I thought we were becoming best friends."

A smirk curls the edge of his lip. "Can we start over? I want to get to know you and I promise I'm not a jerk all the time."

"Is being a jerk just your weekend job?" I shoot back, and his smirk deepens into a smile. "You were such an asshole yesterday. Dracula was minding his own business, and you picked a fight with him. Why?"

The muscles work hard in Loki's face as he clenches his jaw. The bell rings in the background and he glances away briefly, a crease forming between his brows.

"We need to go," he says, and a little part of me is disappointed; I wanted to hear his reply. He trains his gaze back on me and holds out a hand. "What do you say, snake girl? Start fresh?"

Behind him, Murie motions me to say yes. Poor dear looks like she's holding her breath in anticipation. Hesitantly, I shake the demigod's hand and his grin heats up my cheeks. However, when he tries to pull away, I yank him closer and bring my lips to his ear.

"I'll give you a second chance not to be a dick, but I'm warning you, Loki, if you call me snake girl again—"

"But I like snakes," he cuts in, his own lips brushing

my ear. "And who knows? One day I might let you pet *my* snake."

"Is that a euphemism?" I ask dryly.

He just winks as he enters the classroom.

"Not even friends for two seconds and he's knocking out dick jokes," I grumble to Murie.

She giggles and tugs me into the room. All the while my heart does a stupid little dance against my rib cage. I've never met a boy who likes snakes before.

Usually, I frighten or disgust them.

The fact that I do neither to Loki makes me smile as I claim the empty desk beside my sister. I barely settle down when the scent of burning leaves invades my senses. A beautiful middle-aged woman in a black velvet dress sweeps into the room.

"Please settle down everyone and allow me to introduce myself," she says, and all eyes turn to her as she marches to the front of the classroom. The bookshelves and desks in here are just as dark as her clothes and the burning smell clearly belongs to her, which means she's a sorceress. Even her eyes and hair are dark purple, with a long white streak that frames her bangs. She tucks it behind her ear and smoothes a hand down her dress, spreading her ruby lips into a warm smile.

"Welcome to your first day at the academy." Her gaze sweeps around the room. "As your Rep One teacher, it's my job to help guide you back into the light. But I also believe there is no harm in embracing a little darkness." A black flame materializes above her palm, growing larger until it forms a small fire. She manipulates the flames so that they are bending and cracking into different gyrating patterns. "Take today's lesson, for example."

The fire snakes around the room and evaporates around a tall object hidden under a dust sheet. Just like the fire evaporated, so does the sheet into a cloud of dust, revealing a huge tapestry with a brass frame. I don't recognize the handsome young man, but Murie seems to as she chokes out a gasp.

"Is that the Picture of Dorian Gray?"

Mrs Morgana smiles at my sister. "Yes, and everyone has been tasked with removing the curse a former acquaintance of Mr Grey has placed on it." In the blink of an eye, she moves to the painting. "With each day that passes, Mr Grey grows older and the painting younger. It's your job to reverse that by the next full moon. Does anyone know the correct spell to use?"

A simple reversal spell obviously isn't going to work here, so I don't bother volunteering. A few others do, however, and for the next few hours, I watch in amusement as they try to reverse the spell. Every time they fail, a wave of magic turns them into an inanimate object. While Mrs Morgana busies herself turning a lamp back into a student, I catch Loki gazing out the window at a lake in the near distance. His face is mostly hidden, but from what I can see he's deep in thought and the thoughts are unpleasant. Curious, I stand from my chair to make my way over to him, but the bell rings and everyone starts to leave.

"Whew, that was intense." Murie grabs her bag, her

face flushed from all the laughing at failed attempts. "Dorian Gray's cursed picture. How fun!"

"Yeah," I agree, slinging my bag over my shoulder and peeling my gaze off Loki. He leaves the classroom without a backward glance. "I just hope none of us get seriously injured trying to remove these curses."

"I don't think they'll be that powerful," Murie tells me as we leave the classroom. "This is still just a school at the end of the day."

"That's the thing, Murie. I was only joking about this place being a prison, but now I'm beginning to wonder if it really is."

She glances at me. "In what way?"

I half shrug at her, lowering my voice as we follow the others down the passageway. "We're only teenagers and we're handling cursed objects not even the teacher wanted to be near. They couldn't give a fuck about our safety."

"Zara," Mrs Morgana calls before we disappear entirely. "Might I have a word?"

I freeze to the spot, wondering if she heard me.

"Good luck," Murie whispers in my ear before she climbs the ladder.

I turn around and head back into the teacher's room. She waves me over to her desk where she's busy opening a drawer.

"I must say, I'm so very honored to be teaching Mr Knightford's daughter," she says softly, dragging out an iron chest and setting it on her desk. "I wonder if perhaps it is the reason this talisman reacted to your presence."

With another wave of her hand, the chest unlocks and peels its lid open. Mrs Morgana reaches in and sets a gold bangle shaped like a serpent on the desk. The instant I look at it, the snake uncoils itself and slithers over to me.

"How interesting," the teacher mutters, watching me instead of the snake. "Your hair has reacted, too."

Too engrossed by the bangle, I don't notice that some of my hair has turned into snakes. They hiss in greeting at the bangle which latches around my wrist before I can pull back. I lift my hand to study it, but now it's just an ordinary, albeit stunning piece of jewelry.

"Where did you find it?" I ask, my gaze fixed on the intricate engravings. They appear to be written in ancient Greek.

"It appeared on my desk yesterday evening," she answers. "I can feel your magic caressing it which tells me it isn't cursed. One would almost think it's being returned to you. Have you seen it before?"

"No." I shake my head absently, running a finger along the now motionless snake. "But it's very beautiful. Are you sure it's okay to keep it?"

The teacher chuckles. "I don't think you have a choice, Miss Eyre. The talisman has chosen you to be its keeper. Some believe that will bring luck and fortune."

"And what do the others believe?" I ask quietly.

She closes the chest with a soft click. "A bad omen." Then, seeing the worry on my face, she adds quickly, "But I do not think that's the case here. I sense no dark magic from it like I do with Mr Grey's painting. To me, it appears perfectly harmless."

Well, isn't that reassuring?

I've got a strange talisman locked around my wrist that I can't seem to get off.

The weirdest thing of all is that I feel a connection to it.

I just don't know why.

"You get an awesome new bracelet on our first day of class," Murie grumbles with only a tinge of envy. "All I get is a bunch of homework."

"If it's any consolation, I can't get the damn thing off," I tell her, having failed all night to remove it. I hold my wrist up with a light shake, hoping to wake the serpent. I can't figure out how to make it come alive again, or what its purpose is, but something tells me it's got something to do with my hair. Ever since I left the Oubliette yesterday, my hair has been static, which is usually a sign that my gorgon side is about to come out. But yet nothing happens. The snake doesn't move, and neither does my hair.

"What's this class about?" I ask Murie as we walk to class.

"Uh..." Murie pulls her crumpled schedule from her bag and smooths out the paper before reading. "*Reparation Two: Growing Herbs for Potions,* including but not limited to the subjects of magical plants, herbology, crystals, tea leaves, scrying, and divination."

"That sounds right up your alley," I say, opening another door.

"Yeah." She slides past me, her lower lip pursed. "Maybe I can ask my spirit guides for help with Gideon's portrait."

"That's a good idea." I stop and glance around, confused as to where we're headed. This almost looks like we're going outside. "Where are we going?"

"Rep Two is just through there." Murie points to the next set of double doors. "It says it's in the greenhouse."

"Ah, that makes more sense. To the greenhouse we go!"

We walk outside and are greeted by a towering glass greenhouse with dirty windows. It looks as old as the castle, if not more so. We take the last two wooden stools at one of the many apothecary tables and settle down. Each table is lined with glass tubes, vials, mortar and pestles, and plenty of other potion-making equipment I'm admittedly unfamiliar with. Maybe this will be exciting. Neither Murie nor I have experimented with this type of potion-making all that much. Our last school was on the coast of Atlantis and focused more on coral plant life than those ashore.

"Good morning, class, and welcome to Rep Two." A tiny woman appears from behind an enormous cauldron and a glowering fog of incense at the front of the room. She's old, like *really* old, with long, wavy grey hair that hangs to her lower back. The colorful skirt flowing around her ankles, complete with her bangles clanging like wind chimes, tells me she's the eccentric kind. "I will be your teacher, Ms. Athame. In this class, we'll be learning potions to help with your other reparation classes. A little birdy told me that you're all currently trying to erase the curse on Mr Grey's portrait. Well, today I'm going to show you how to create a simple, yet highly effective potion that will momentarily reverse the effects of the curse. It'll be up to you to create a potion similar to this that will achieve the result long-term."

The door to the greenhouse creaks open. We all turn to see who's arrived late, and to my dismay, it's Hades.

"Ah," Ms Athame says. "Hello. You are late."

"Sorry." He shrugs before noticing me, a lopsided grin pulling at his lips. He notices the only remaining stool, the one on my left, and his grin turns into a full-blown smile.

"Well, don't just stand there catching flies." Ms. Athame motions for him to sit down. "Go ahead and take a seat."

When Hades nears me, the snake around my wrist softens and glows. I nudge Murie and point to my wrist. Hades pulls the stool out and sits down, causing the snake to twist its head to look at him. All three of us look at him. He smiles down at the snake and then to me. Before I know it, the snake hardens back into my bracelet. What the ever-loving fuck was that all about? Why did my bracelet react to Hades?

"Now we can begin." Ms Athame claps her hands and approaches the smoking cauldron.

She whispers a spell and starts to throw in a bunch of ingredients. It's hard to keep up with what any of them are. She explains mixing potions is part ingredients, part spellcasting, and the rest is comprised of one's intentions and intuitions.

Murie and I scribble notes in our books as we watch her. I glance at Hades every so often and notice how comfortable he looks. Has he taken this class before? Or was potion making something he did as a hobby? I'm not sure, but I do notice he isn't taking any notes and seems to be following along with ease. Another thing I notice is how amazing he smells, which irritates me. I shouldn't be focusing on that. I shouldn't even be sneaking looks at him… yet I am. Even the snake-bracelet-thingy seems to be focused on him.

"Alright, before we end today's class," the teacher says, clapping her hands to grab our attention, "who would like to volunteer to come up and try to recreate what I just demonstrated?"

My hand shoots up before my brain can properly assess the possible repercussions of my actions. Murie looks at me, wide-eyed as an owl.

"What are you doing?" she hisses in a whisper. "You followed along with all that?"

I look up at my hand, half-unaware that I had shot it up. My face flushes with heat. Hades grins at me, arms folded across his chest, and I know there's no turning back.

"Fantastic!" Ms. Athame applauds again, her eyes

sweeping around the greenhouse. "And who will be her partner?"

I look at Murie, but it's too late. Hades puts up his hand.

"I will," he says, standing without even looking at me.

I try to burn a hole into the back of his head with my eyes, but nothing happens.

"Perfect!" Ms Athame waves me over. "Come on up, dear."

I let out an audible sigh, directed at Hades, and scoot my stool back. I walk up to the cauldron and stand beside Hades, who looks positively fucking delighted with himself. As I stare into the cauldron, the blood suddenly drains from my face as my mind goes blank. I have no idea what to do. Why the hell did I put my hand up?

"I'll start," Hades says, stepping around me. He grabs some spices, whispers a spell, and throws them in. The contents hiss and react, much to the delight of the teacher.

"Great!" She wafts some of the smoke into her face and sighs with approval. "Now, Miss Eyre."

"Umm, I..." I lamely stammer, glancing at the vials on the table. I can't recall what she did next, so I pick up one with feigned confidence and throw it in, hoping for the best.

"No, not that!" Hades covers his face with his arms as a small explosion bursts from the cauldron, sending up a flare of sparks.

"Oh, shit!" I fumble and grab what I think is water off the table, throwing it in.

I hear Ms Athame screaming over the chaos, but it's too late. Thick smoke billows from the cauldron and black flames lick around the outer rim. The contents inside gather to the edge, seconds from brimming over.

"What have you done?" Hades seizes my wrists to stop me from grabbing something else off the table. "You'll just make it worse."

"Don't you touch me," I warn, shrugging him off.

Ms. Athame runs over with water and tosses it into the swaying cauldron. The flames die with a deafening hiss, but the smoke still remains filling up the greenhouse.

"You could've killed us," Hades hisses in a whisper.

"I said let go of me!" I practically scream the words out, thrashing so hard that I not only free myself of his grip, but I also fling him into the side of the cauldron. Clearly pushing him into things is becoming a habit. He knocks the cauldron over and all hell breaks loose.

The students erupt into chaos and run out of the greenhouse, including Murie, as the bubbling liquid oozes over the floor and equipment. I stand frozen in place, looking at what just happened, while Ms Athame helps Hades to his feet.

Oh, shit… I've gone and done it again.

"I will *not* tolerate this kind of behavior in my class!" For such a small old woman, Ms Athame can be a little terrifying when she's pissed off. "Mr Erebus, Miss Eyre, I want you to go out to the forest and replace the ingredients you have so carelessly destroyed. You will go *together* and work as a *team*. Understood?"

"But—" I begin to protest.

"Is that understood?" she snaps, her features hardening.

"Yes." Hades gets to his feet and makes eye contact with me, a silent plea to shut the hell up and agree.

Grumbling under my breath, I give a silent nod and rise to my feet.

"Can you give us a list, Ms Athame?" Hades asks softly.

The teacher writes down the ingredients on a small scroll and gives it to Hades. I only recognize one of the three—the Deadly Moonflower. The herb and mushroom don't ring a bell, but apparently Hades knows, so when we enter the forest, I follow him without protest.

"She said they aren't hard to find," he reminds me for the third time, leaning down to inspect something in the dirt.

"Did you find one?" I ask, eager to just get this whole thing over with.

"Nah." He stands and looks at me with a smile. "Not what I thought it was."

"Then why are you smiling?" I ask when he doesn't look away.

"Not even going to say sorry, huh?"

I frown at him. "Sorry for what?"

He steps closer to me, his scent invading my senses. "Knocking me over, for starters."

"Ha! That's rich. You should be the one apologizing to me."

He furrows his brow. "What am I apologizing for? I didn't explode the potion."

"No, but you did hold me down. That's twice you've grabbed me without my consent. Has no one taught you that's not okay?"

He worries his lower lip for a moment, his amber eyes searching mine.

"You're right," he says with a nod. "I'm sorry and I will be more careful."

That catches me off guard. Actually, I didn't expect him to apologize, and I'm certainly not going to because I didn't do anything wrong. I just shrugged him off. It's not my fault his clumsy ass fell into the cauldron. If he didn't touch me, he wouldn't have knocked the cauldron over.

I decide to change the subject by asking, "What are you in here for, anyway?"

He rummages through some shrubbery, plucks a leaf, and inspects it. "Found the herb. Only two ingredients left."

"Are you just going to ignore my question?" I bend down to inspect a mushroom. It looks like the picture, so I pluck a handful and sweep them into my bag. "Got the mushrooms. Now we just need the flower."

"You know why I'm in here," Hades replies, following me this time. "Don't act like you haven't heard."

"You freed a bunch of criminals," I say, more of a statement than a question.

"Is that what you heard?" He falls into step with me. "And is that why you have a problem with me?"

I shrug. "We haven't gotten off to the best start."

"No, we haven't, but it was entirely my fault." He's silent for a moment, only the sounds of leaves crunching under his boots for company. "The criminal thing you mentioned? That's not what happened. I didn't mean to free them, I was just..." He searches for his words, and I peek at him through my lashes, surprised by the pained look on his face. "I was looking for something important." His eyes meet mine. "Something that was taken from me."

I nod as we walk further into the forest, the two of us falling into a surprisingly comfortable silence. I never would've thought I'd be enjoying a walk with the guy I knocked into a lake on my first day at the academy, but here we are. And the worse thing is that I'm not as desperate to get away from him. There's something about Hades that feels strangely familiar. I haven't met him before, contrary to what he thinks, but there is something I can't quite put my finger on.

When shadows grow darker around us, my bracelet starts to glow up like a torch.

"Woah, check this out."

I hold out my wrist, and Hades is just as intrigued as I am.

The snake glows brighter the more we walk in one direction, so we continue down the path until we reach an opening right at the edge of the island. The entire field is covered in flowers the same color as Hades' hair.

"Hey, look at that. It's the flower." Hades leans down

and plucks the final ingredient from the ground. "Looks like we've got them all."

"Finally," I mutter, though my bracelet is vibrating as well as glowing. I walk through the flowers to stand with Hades, and the closer I get, the harder it vibrates. "I think it's trying to tell us something."

"The dirt here is fresh," Hades says, digging through the soil around where he plucked the flower. "Do you think your bracelet is reacting to something in the ground?"

"Could be. Let's find out."

I lean down with him and dig through the soil.

Hades pauses when the helm of something pokes out from the surface.

I watch him drag it out, and to my amazement, it's a beautiful gold scythe not much bigger than my arm. The soil falls away like melted snow when he lifts it up to inspect it in the sunlight. The second I reach out to touch it, a bolt of lightning surges into my body, almost shocking me out of my skin.

It feels like only a minute later when I come to in Hades' arms, his worried face hanging over me. I can see his lips moving but I struggle to find my breath let alone a reply.

"I'm fine," I manage to say after a moment, shrugging him off as I rise unsteadily to my feet. I don't know what the hell that was, but I'm not about to look weak in front of him. I try to put on a brave face despite the unease taking root inside of me. "We should head back."

A crease forms between his brows. "But what the hell was that?"

"I… I don't know."

"I think I do." He taps his lower lip in thought. "Something like that happened to me once back at the Paranormal Crime Unit."

Now that piques my interest despite my sudden exhaustion. "Really? What was it?" I ask.

He hesitates only briefly. "I'm not sure, but I know who we can ask."

"Mrs Morgana?" I offer, glancing at my bracelet; the snake is no longer moving or glowing, its purpose served...for now.

With a nod from Hades, we head back to the academy.

CHAPTER SIX

The journey back to the greenhouse feels longer than I remember. Maybe it's because I feel so weak now. With every step, the weakness turns into complete and utter exhaustion. Hades holds the scythe while I carry the ingredients in my bag as we walk back through the murky greenhouse doors. The class is empty and Ms. Athame stands sweeping the last of the mess from around the cauldron. She looks up at us expectantly, reading our energy.

"You found them! So soon? What happened? Are you okay?" She assesses me as I gently lay down the ingredients on the table. She nods at them with approval, but her beady eyes remain pressed on us for an answer. "Well?"

"Yes, we're okay," I answer, just managing to hold back a yawn.

"We're sorry again," Hades adds hurriedly, "but we have to go now. We need to see Mrs Morgana."

He sweeps out of the room before Ms Athame can

stop him. With an apologetic smile at her, I leave and hurry after him toward the Oubliette. Hades climbs down first, and when I land beside him, we find Mrs Morgana just entering her classroom.

I call out her name and she pauses in the doorway, turning to us.

"What is the mat…" Her gaze lands on the scythe in Hades' arms, and her eyes widen into saucers. "That object you carry holds tremendous power."

"It's what we've come to speak to you about," Hades says, holding out the scythe. "Whatever this is reacted to Zara's bracelet. Or maybe it was the other way around. We're not sure."

She grimaces at the scythe and then looks at me, inspecting my face. "Are you feeling alright?"

"Something happened when I touched it," I tell her, rubbing a strange chill from my arms. "I've felt exhausted ever since."

"Come in and tell me exactly what happened," she says, pivoting on her heel.

We follow her into the classroom and I lean against the desk I sat at yesterday. Hades claims the one beside me.

"My bracelet reacted like Hades said," I start off quietly. "We were gathering ingredients for Ms Athame and had to go a little further out to find the last one we needed. We came to an opening at the end of the forest, a field covered in flowers."

She nods thoughtfully. "Yes, that would be Moon-flower Meadow. It's near the cliff on the edge of the island."

"That's it. Well, my bracelet started to light up and vibrate the closer I got to the meadow. We found a patch of dirt that looked soft and fresh, so we started to dig, and that's when we found the scythe. When I reached out for it…"

"Go on," Mrs Morgana encourages me softly. "It's okay, Zara. You can tell me what happened." She reaches out to place a hand on mine and offers a reassuring smile. "And once you do, you must rest. I will arrange for Doctor Jekyll to give you a checkup. You look on the verge of passing out."

"Really, I'm okay." Another yawn catches me and I hide it behind my hand. "Anyway, when I touched the scythe, I was given an electric shock."

"Electric shock is putting it mildly," Hades cuts in. "She flew backward and was knocked out for at least ten minutes. Her whole body was convulsing."

I point at the scythe, keeping my distance from it. "We wanted to ask if you know what this scythe is. Hades said he experienced something similar once before."

He nods grimly. "I felt the curse hit me the second I touched it. I was drained for days after. Seeing her react the way she did reminded me of that, of what I felt, and I wonder if it's similar and that maybe it's cursed."

"Is that the scythe?" Mr. Knightford asks, his voice startling us. He strides into the classroom, his eyes rooted on the scythe. "Let me see it."

Hades hands the weapon to him, and we watch the headmaster—*my dad*—pore over it in silence.

"While I don't know anything about this relic," Mrs Morgana says, "it seems the man who does just showed up." She smiles at Mr. Knightford, but he's too focused on the scythe to look at her.

"Yes, these are ancient relics." He turns the scythe over in his palm, assessing every inch of it. The gold metal gleams in his eyes like a beacon of sunlight. "They only react to those whose powers are on par with its own."

I exchange a worried glance with Hades.

"What kind of relics are they?" I ask.

Mr Knightford peels his gaze off the object and looks at me. "This scythe is one of four ancient relics known as The Gilded Four. They belonged to the Four Horsemen, Conquest, War, Famine and Death, who desired more than anything to use these weapons to bring about the apocalypse. They buried each one on the island, but no living creature knows their location." He admires the scythe once more, the crescent blade glinting under the light. "When all four of them are united, power unlike anything you could imagine will be born, which can then be used to protect the entire island."

"If the relics were so important to begin with, why were they buried?" Hades takes the words straight out of my mouth. "Why did the Four Horsemen hide them?"

"Because their adversaries kept trying to steal them to prevent the apocalypse," Mr Knightford explains, his eyebrows knitting together. "But we can protect them better now with stronger spells, which in turn will protect the academy." He looks at me, then at my bracelet. "Did it react to you? Is that how you found it?"

"My bracelet reacted to it and led us to Moonflower Meadow."

"What were you doing all the way out there?" The concern in his voice is palpable, almost like that of an overprotective father.

"Looking for replacement ingredients for Ms Athame. We... had an accident," Hades smoothly answers, eyeing me closely.

If Mr Knightford has more to say on the matter, he doesn't voice it. "And did you, Hades, have a reaction to the relic?"

"No, but I have reacted to objects in a similar way in the past."

Mr Knightford smacks his lips together, sliding me a veiled glance. "Yes, I know." He looks between us and then to the scythe. "I believe you two may be our best chance."

"For what?" Hades asks, crossing his arms over his leather jacket.

"Finding the other three; a bow, hammer, and sword. You both have experienced reactions to magical objects in the past. That means you have a better chance of finding the relics since they will call out to you. Yes, that is it. It's decided. You will find the other relics for me together."

"Why together? Hades didn't react to the scythe," I protest, not wanting to spend more time with Hades than I need to.

"That may be so," Mr Knightford says, "but Hades

may react to another one that you might not. That is why you both need to work as a team if we want to find the other relics and protect the island."

Without a flicker of hesitation, Hades nods. "Count me in."

I gawk at him, then Mrs Morgana, and lastly my fath... Mr Knightford. I thought he understood how I felt about Hades.

So much for having 'words' with him.

"Fine," I mutter reluctantly, looking away from Hades.

"Thank you both," Mr Knightford says, his gaze still on the scythe as if it's the greatest thing in existence. "Please do keep me updated on your progress. And don't worry. I will hold on to the scythe until the others have been collected..."

CHAPTER SEVEN

The next day is Magical Defense with our substitute teacher, Miss Torrigan. This is my second reparation class without Murie, which really sucks because I wanted her with me in this one more than the others. Once we're all dressed in our workout clothes, we gather on the back field that overlooks the edge of the island. I guess this field is the closest thing the academy's got to a gym.

My first week at the academy isn't even over yet and so much has happened. I'm actually relieved to let off some steam.

According to Miss Torrigan, we'd normally be doing magical activities that involve exercise, but since Mr Erebus is off sick, Miss Torrigan says we can play soccer ball. I stand by the edge of the field, watching everyone chasing after the ball. It's strange to watch them play a human sport as if we're not locked up in this prison.

Dracula runs past me with a big grin stretching

over his lips. "What's the matter, Zara? Never played soccer before?"

I rove my gaze over his tight grey tee and blood-red shorts. I lick my lips at the sight of him. Damn, he looks hot. I've always been a sucker for the lean athletic type and Dracula is exactly that. Of course, there's also nothing wrong with a little bad boy every now and then.

"Not my game," I say, throwing Dracula a flirtatious smile. Why am I suddenly so attracted to a vampire? Maybe it really is the "bad boy" part of it. Being *The* Dracula's son just adds to his sex appeal. What would kissing and fucking Dracula's son be like?

For a moment, I'm lost within the blissful reverie, and Dracula moves away. I watch him run down the end of the field, turn, and kick the ball with tremendous force. It flies towards me and I move out of the way at the last second, just managing to dodge it.

A flash of disappointment flits over Dracula's face. The damn vampire is trying to give me a concussion! The others run past me in pursuit of the ball. I never did understand this sport. Or any sport. They aren't really my thing, and until now, I thought only humans played them. I pretend to look bored as Dracula charges across the field and back up to me.

He stands by my side silently with the faintest grin tugging the left side of his mouth.

I examine my nails, pretending not to see him. He's lucky I don't use magic to throw the ball into his handsome face.

"Must be pretty interesting."

"What was that?" I keep looking at my fingers and he chuckles under his breath.

"Your nails," he says after a moment.

I keep my gaze cast downward, seriously considering hitting him with the ball. "Not hard to be more interesting than soccer." I look up to meet his gaze. "Or you."

This lights a fire in him. He loves it like I knew he would. "Oh, is that so?" His lips spread into a grin. "Not interested in that?" He juts his chin toward the ball at the far end of the field, then gets closer to me and whispers, "Or me, my inimă?"

"Maybe. Maybe not." I shrug my shoulder, unable to restrain my smirk. "Maybe go fuck yourself."

"I mean..." He takes a step back, pretending what I said didn't just give him a hard on. Gods, he's so easy. And I love teasing him like this. "I was about to ask you to a party."

Now he's got my attention. "A party?" I ask.

"Until you told me to go fuck myself. Which I will. Thinking of you." He slides his tongue across his fangs and I feel a rush of blood gathering between my legs.

I can play this game, too. "Party was probably going to be lame, anyway."

He shakes his head, still smirking at me. "Parties here are pretty legit. And if you and I go? It's guaranteed to be a good time."

"Oh, really?" I arch a brow at him.

He merely winks. "Would I lie to you?"

Usually ego turns me off, but when Dracula does it,

I can't resist the arousal gathering inside me. To my utter surprise, I find myself nodding.

"You're right. The two of us can make any scene more interesting," I say, gesturing my hands around the field.

"Precisely. We're sexing up this lame ass soccer field. But it's all beside the point now, because you told me to go fuck myself. Consider the invitation revoked."

I cross my arms and glare at him playfully. "You didn't invite me to begin with."

His mouth opens and then shuts it again. "You've got me there." He puts a hand to his chin. "How about this? We play this dumb ass soccer game to pass the time. I score a point before you, you come to the party with me. You score a point before me, I fuck myself and fly solo."

There's that name again. I ignore it and consider his proposal. I hate this game and now I really want to go to that party, so as long as I let him score first, it's a win/win for me. I don't even have to try. I think he knows this, and it's why he proposed it.

I stick my hand out to shake. "Deal."

He accepts it with a grin, his fangs gleaming in the sunlight. "Deal."

And then he runs after the ball, and I pretend to care. In less than a minute he's gotten it away from our classmates and down the field. I half-assedly try to stop him, but he kicks the ball so hard it shoots over my head and lifts my hair before landing in the goal. He laughs as he makes his way back over to me.

"Oh shoot. Now I have to go to the party with you," I say, shrugging innocently.

He laughs again. "You didn't even pretend to try."

"Didn't I? I thought I was pretty convincing."

He shakes his head. "Nah. But it doesn't matter. I got what I wanted, which is you, my inimă."

The bell sounds and everyone runs from the fields back towards the locker rooms. Dracula and I take our time, wanting to walk and be alone.

"Why do you call me that?" I ask.

"What?"

"My inimă. What is that? Is it actually Romanian?"

"It's an English translation of *inimă mea*, which basically means 'my heart'."

"You've called me it a few times now. Why?"

He thinks for a moment, almost like he's wondering if he should tell me. "Well, first of all, vampires don't have hearts."

"That I already know," I blurt out, not wanting him to think I'm stupid.

"Right. So when we find someone we consider our soulmate, we call them inimă because their heart beats for the two of us."

Despite the flutter my heart gives, I scrunch my face up at him. "That is so damn cheesy."

He chuckles quietly. "Once we find a mate and drink their blood, it connects us. Your blood is mine. Your heart is ours. It makes us both come alive. So, yes, we believe in soul mates, because without them, we live only half a life."

We stop walking and as much as I hate to admit it,

that line works on me. I feel like he's being genuine and I find myself interested in him more and more. "I usually hate romantic shit like that," I confess. "But that was actually pretty cute and heartfelt."

"Well, it's the truth. It's how I feel about you. You're my inimă, and only my inimă gets to call me Drac," he adds with a wink.

My cheeks heat up as we come to a stop outside the locker rooms. No one is around us. I feel something pulsate the air between us and I don't want the moment to end.

"When is the party, by the way?"

"This weekend out in the forest."

"Can you be more specific?" I ask.

"So many questions." He puts a hand on the wall behind me, real high school movie like, and leans in. I don't fight it. I love it. I want it. I want *him*. His lips are cold as they meet mine. Our chests meld and I hope he can feel my heartbeat. I'm so turned on by all of this I want to fuck him right here in the halls.

He pulls back with a smile. "Friday. I'll pick you up at six, my little inimă."

"Sure thing, my little dork."

We both laugh before parting ways. That vampire is really starting to worm his way into my heart.

Dammit.

CHAPTER EIGHT

As soon as classes are over and I get back to my dorm room, I tell Murie about the party.

"It sounds wicked but I've already got plans with Kal," she says, her features pulling into a frown. "Sorry, Zee."

I mask my disappointment with a smile and continue putting on my lipstick in the bathroom mirror. In all honesty, I've missed hanging out with my sister. We're just busy spending time with other people and that's totally okay. It happens. It also makes me smile to know we're both falling for vampires.

I have not personally gotten to know Kal yet, but Murie certainly has and every time she talks about him she blushes or pulls that far off, dreamy expression. It's a little cute to see her crushing on Wrath's Head Boy. I don't think I've ever seen her like this before.

"Where is the party, anyway?" Murie asks, sliding next to me and putting on a lilac lipstick.

"I'm not sure. Somewhere out in the forest, I think."

Her eyebrows lift, and she pauses putting on her lipstick. "Sorry, for a minute there I thought you said you were going to a party out in the forest."

I nudge her shoulder with mine. "I'll be fine. Drac wasn't very specific when he told me the details."

Murie breathes through her nose and scoffs. "Yeah because that doesn't sound shady at all." She finishes her makeup and tucks the lipstick into the pocket of her sequin dress. "Mum would whip your ass with all six tentacles if she knew this."

A quiet giggle escapes me. "Don't worry. I trust Drac."

"But you barely know him," she counters, her expression sobering. She's no longer laughing and is deadly serious now. "What if he assaults you?"

I can't help but cringe at the word. "I understand your concern, but seriously, I feel safe with him even if he acts like an idiot sometimes. And anyway, I should be the one worried about you! What if Kal tries to take advantage of you?"

She just shrugs at me. "Then I've got six tentacles to punch him with."

"I think you'll find I'm not that kinda guy," Kal says, his face pulled into a frown as he appears in the doorway to our room. He looks directly at Murie. "I'd sooner kill anyone who wishes to inflict harm on my babygirl."

Murie smiles at him and blushes. Sure enough, the moment she sees him, she's all lovestruck again. I'm surprised she hasn't got cartoon hearts beating out from her eyes.

"Jeez! I didn't know you were standing there," I say to Kal, pressing a hand to my chest in exaggeration. "Pretty darn sneaky." I face Murie with an arched brow. "Like a rapist."

"Woah, woah, woah." He holds up his hands in defense. "What's all this talk about rape? And why am I involved?"

I shoot Murie a mock glare. "She's the one who brought it up."

Kal looks at her, his eyebrows snapping together. "What!? You did?"

"No!" Murie buries her head in her hands with exasperation. "Not like that. Not about you. This is a misunderstanding!"

Kal walks over to Murie's bed, sits on the edge, and taps the space next to him. "Explain it to me then, please."

Murie remains standing in front of the mirror, her face turning more beet red by the second. Hopefully she translates my silent glare as to not tell Kal about the party.

"I was talking about Dracula. Zara's going to a party with him in the forest."

"Damn it, Murie!" I stomp my foot and shove my lipstick into my purse.

"Telling him kind of defeats the purpose of it being a secret or me sneaking out."

Kal just laughs as if it's all a big joke. "That party is not a secret."

"It's not?" I ask, drawing my eyebrows together.

"No, everyone knows about it. Literally everyone."

"Then why did Drac say we need to sneak out?"

"Because people still try to be discreet, but it's something we all know is happening." Kal waves a hand dismissively. "Kind of one of those unspoken things."

"Huh," is all I can say as I try to figure out why Dracula was so secretive about the party.

"So, Murie," Kal says, turning to my sister who still hasn't budged from the mirror. "What does this party have to do with me or rape?"

Murie's blush deepens. "Well, I was just saying that going into the forest for a party with a vampire she barely knows is a bad idea. She replied that it was just as much a bad idea as our, err, date tonight. But she was just kidding. Weren't you, Zee?"

I watch the dark expression drifting over Kal's face. It's a combination of shock, horror, and disgust all twisted into one. His mouth falls open, and he shakes his head before looking in my direction.

"You really think that of me?" he asks quietly.

"No, I was joking. But if you do hurt my sister, I won't think twice about turning you into stone."

"I see." Kal stands from the bed, his muscles turning rigid. "That isn't something you should joke about, Zara."

Murie moves beside him and takes his hand. "Agreed."

Et tu, Murie?

"What?! You're the one who said it first, about Drac," I shout at her, but she doesn't have a chance to open her mouth.

"What about me?" Dracula asks, entering the room

dressed in a dark grey, three-piece suit with a crimson cravat. Gods, he looks handsome.

"Is the whole appearing in doorways a vampire thing?" I ask, scrunching my face at him.

Dracula exchanges a glance with Kal. "We are known for our surreptitious nature."

"Alright, let's just get out of here." I walk over to him, grinning. "Ready to go?"

"I'm ready, my inimă." He slides his gaze over me slowly, his eyes widening as though he enjoys the view of my black lace dress. "You look amazing."

"Thank you." I step closer and almost lean in to kiss him when I remember Murie and Kal are right behind us. I turn to them, asking softly, "Are you sure you don't want to come to the party?"

"It'll be a blast," Dracula adds, wiggling his eyebrows suggestively.

Kal nods grimly. "I'm sure. They're not really my thing."

"Me either. But you two have fun," Murie says, winking at me as we leave the room.

"How do we get to the party since it's past curfew?" I ask Dracula.

He flashes me a wolfish grin. "I found a hidden door that leads straight into the forest. Honestly. It's like Knightford wants us to break his rules."

"You're such a bad boy," I tease, quietly following him down the hallway.

Instead of leaving the dorms, Dracula leads me into a maintenance closet that isn't a closet at all. It's a small room that hides a narrow staircase. At the very bottom of it, we step out into another room containing only a single door carved into the granite wall. Dracula opens it and motions for me to go first.

The cool night air sweeps over me as I step out into the twilight. As soon as Dracula reaches my side, he takes my hand in his, the ruby on his ring blinking up at me.

"What is the ring for?"

Dracula follows my gaze to our joined hands. "This is how I can walk about in the sun. It's something only ancient vampires have. Those who don't have it risk burning. And no, they don't combust, but they do burn like a bitch."

"Are you ancient?" I ask, curious about his history. I don't really know much about him other than he has history with Loki and that his dad is Count Dracula.

"I'm part of an ancient bloodline," he answers, then nodding at the gate: "Just through here and there should be a portal that will take us to the party."

After a short stroll through the forest, we arrive at the portal. If not for the smell of burning magic radiating from the carved out tree drunk, I'd almost completely miss it. Dracula guides me through and on the other side, we step into a moonlight-soaked meadow filled with people dancing around a gorging fire. Crystals hang from the trees dotted around the clearing and the music is loud, transmitted through speaks that hover in the air above us.

"It's a bonafide rager," I say to Dracula, smiling at him. "Time to get our freak on!"

He just laughs and nods to the table laden with

plastic cups and bottles of alcohol. "Would you like a drink first?"

"Make it a double. I'm feeling badass tonight."

Again he chuckles, and the sound is endearing to hear. I wish he'd laugh like this more. He returns a few minutes later with a drink for me, which I hesitate before accepting; I don't know why but I trust Dracula. As I sip the sweet alcohol, I sweep my gaze around the clearing. I don't recognize anyone here, which is a good thing. I throw back the last of my drink, and after a couple more, I'm ready to dance.

So I drag my vampire date onto the dance floor despite his protests.

"I take it you have a low tolerance to alcohol?"

I spin around, moving my body to the music. "Whaddaya mean?"

Dracula arches a brow at me, pointing to my drink which I *may* have spilled on my dress. "I think you've had enough for now."

He reaches out to take my cup and I stumble back, lifting my arm away from him. "Hey, hey! I'm not..." I stop to hiccup, then grin at him. "...d-drunk. I have an extremely-ly high tolerance."

His hand falls to my waist as he spins me around. "Really?"

"Uh-huh. Promise."

When I almost fall onto my ass, Dracula holds me closer. "I'm going to get you some water. Try not to hurt yourself while I'm gone, okay?"

"Yup," I say, extending my empty cup to him.

He takes it and walks back to the drink table. A new

song comes on, a heavy electronic beat. I can't remember the last time I was able to let go like this. So I shut my eyes and fall into the rhythm of the song, completely lost to the music. It's not until a hand wraps around my bare waist do I stop. I turn around into the embrace, thinking it's Dracula, but when I open my eyes, Loki grins down at me like an idiot.

For some reason, his close proximity doesn't bother me. Maybe it's the music. Maybe it's the alcohol. I am in too good of a mood to be brought down, which is why I decide to just dance with him.

"Damn, you're a hot dancer," he says in my ear, his breath trickling down the side of my neck.

"Thanks."

"You're all anyone can look at."

"Mmhmm." I turn and rock my body against his, my arms lifted in the air again.

"Even Hades can't stop looking at you."

Now that catches my attention. "What? Hades?"

I follow Loki's gaze off to a corner of the crowd where Hades stands alone in a black tux. He looks away the moment we make eye contact and runs a hand through his slicked back, blue hair.

"Like I said," Loki whispers, his hand warm against the small of my back. "You're all anyone can look at."

"And she's here with me." Dracula stands in front of us, holding two cups. "Here you go, my inimă."

I take the cup and sip the water. The way he's caring for me is ridiculously sexy. "Thank you," I tell him, and then looking at Loki, I say, "And thank you for the dance."

"Please, the pleasure was all mine." Loki winks at and then offers Dracula a hard stare before stalking off.

By the time I finish the water, I still feel sufficiently drunk and sick from the fast movements of my dancing. "What time is it?"

Dracula glances at his watch. "Past one A.M."

"Oh." I look around the meadow, my vision slightly unsteady. "I feel a bit sick."

"Want to go?" He raises a suggestive eyebrow at me.

I nod, and with a smile, he intertwines his fingers with mine. We make our way through the portal and during the short walk through the forest. I realize how dangerously dark it is here with only slivers of moonlight here and there.

A rustling noise in the darkness halts my steps.

"What is it?" Dracula asks, glancing around us.

"Didn't you hear that?"

For a moment, we just stand in the near darkness straining our senses. But it's impossible to see anything out here no matter how heightened my gorgon side makes my vision.

"Let's get out of here," Dracula says, leading the way through the forest at a brisk pace.

The rustling noise carries to my ears again, this time followed by snapping twigs.

Okay. This totally feels like some cliche horror movie scene.

And when I catch the red eyes flitting between the shadows of the trees, I almost laugh if not for the fear that snakes into me and snatches the air from my lungs. Before I can so much as defend myself, a creature covered in blood jumps out at me. Its clawed hands seize into my shoulders, and in one fluid movement, pins me to the ground. The blood in its mouth oozes down onto my face, and I scream like I've never screamed before.

"Get the fuck away from her!"

Dracula's screams are just as deafening as he pounces onto the rabid vampire and sinks his fangs into its neck like a wolf catching its prey. The creature roars and tries to fling him off, but Dracula hacks into its throat like a slice of meat and then hauls it off me. With a twist of his hand, he snaps the creature's neck and then throws its corpse to the ground. My heart thrashes in my chest like wild pistons and Dracula's chest rises unevenly, his eyes a deep, shining red.

"My inimă, are you okay?" He bends down to help me up, but I stay still for a moment, more out of shock than anything at the near-death experience. "Are you injured?"

"No, I'm okay. I just can't believe I was frozen like that."

He shakes his head. "You were in shock. But don't worry. I've got you, my inimă."

My pulse accelerates every damn time he calls me his heart. It's so silly to get all lovestruck over it, and yet I love it. Roughly grabbing his hand, I pull him down onto the ground with me and crash my mouth to his. His lips are softer than expected and cold against my flushed skin.

When he tries to pull away and lift me to my feet, I shove him onto his back so that I can straddle his hips.

His hardened cock presses against me, and gods, it already feels wonderful.

"Zara…" My name barely leaves his lips on a whisper. "What are you doing?"

I smile down at him, hiding my necklace underneath my shirt. "I want to thank you."

"You don't need to thank me," he counters with a frown.

"Okay. Then I want to fuck you."

His pupils dilate as I lift my hips a little and pull my panties aside. I reach down and stroke his cock through the silk material, then I unzip him and pull him out. He holds his breath as he looks up at me, and with the moonlight bathing him in a silver hue, he looks more translucent than ever before. His eyes are like hypnotic pools of molten rubies and I can't look away from them when I slide down onto his cock.

Gods, he feels amazing inside me. I want to take him slowly, but with the adrenaline still coursing through my body, my movements are frantic, frenzied by my lust for him. I knew this vampire had wormed his way into my heart, but I never thought I'd be fucking him in the middle of the forest after nearly being killed.

I've heard that some vampires can turn rabid like the one that attacked me, but I never thought I'd have the misfortune of encountering one. Thank goodness Dracula was here, or I'd pretty much be pushing up daisies.

With his bravery playing through my mind, I rock

back and forth on his cock, our gaze never leaving each other.

He rests his hands on my hips and guides me down, his head tilted back as another moan escapes him.

I lean down and smother them with my lips.

His hand gently fists my hair as he pulls me closer and a loose strand tangles around his ring.

"My inimă," he whispers against my mouth, our faces bathed in the moonlight.

Stars dance over my line of sight as I close my eyes, succumbing to the pleasure that tingles through me. It's not long before the sensation bursts into a shattering orgasm that has me arching my spine and screaming out his name.

I look down at him, and his fangs extend even more, glinting in the near darkness.

His eyes shimmer like molten rubies as he gazes back up at me, his lips slightly parted, and then he's coming.

I orgasm again, loving the sensation of his cock pulsing inside me, and this time Dracula leans forward and runs his fangs down the valley of my throat.

For a moment, I almost think he's about to bite me, but he clenches his eyes and sucks a breath in through his nose. My body trembles with the aftershocks of pleasure and I carefully get to my feet, my legs almost liquefying beneath me. I keep my feet planted at either side of Dracula and he looks up at me as I pull my panties up. His lips quirk into a grin that makes my heart skip a beat.

"You look more beautiful than in my dreams," he

says, his fangs returning to their usual length. "I almost couldn't restrain myself."

"Restrain yourself from what?" I ask, untucking my necklace and moving aside so that he can stand up.

He's quiet for a moment while he adjusts himself. It's then I become deathly aware of our vulnerable situation. Naked in the woods, after nearly being killed by a rapid creature, is definitely not the wisest decision I've ever made.

As if reading my thoughts, Dracula turns to me and holds out his hand. "Let's go home."

My heart clenches at the word home. The Academy for Villains will never be my home, but with Dracula here, it no longer feels like a prison.

Taking my hand firmly in his, Dracula leads me through the forest with me held close at his side. It's not until the academy is within reach does he answer my question from before.

"One of the reasons my father and I don't get along is because I refuse to drink human blood. Back there..." He trails off, and I squeeze his hand in reassurance. He bites his lip before releasing it. "I almost couldn't control myself." His eyes flash toward mine and there's a darkness in them I've never seen before. "Can you forgive me?"

In all honesty, my stomach churns at the thought of him drinking blood from me. It's not really something I've ever thought about it. But the pained look on his face, coupled with the fact that he clearly doesn't want to hurt me, settles my unease. I find myself wondering what it would actually feel like.

"There's nothing to forgive," I say, sliding through the academy gate. "You didn't bite me without my consent."

"No, I didn't." A muscle in his jaw twitches as he looks up at the crescent moon nestled in the inky-black sky. "But I wanted to. Gods, I wanted to. I almost hate myself as much as that vampire who attacked you."

I stop and press a kiss to his lips, before saying, "You'd never hurt me. Besides, who knows? Maybe I won't mind letting you taste me in the future." I finish with a wink that makes Dracula smirk.

"It would be an honor to drink from you and bind our hearts," he says, his tone so serious that it makes me blush a little.

I'm actually lost for words and decide to stay quiet as we sneak back into the academy. Dracula can be so embarrassingly sincere and romantic that I'm not quite sure what to make of it.

Once we step out of the maintenance closet, Miss Torrigan is waiting for us with at least seven other students she's caught already. Her unusual eyes meet mine and she shakes her head, almost like that of a disappointed mother.

"Zara, I expected better from you," she says, and I frown at her. Now she really sounds like my mother, and something about that rubs me the wrong way. I've seen how she looks at Mr Knightford, all bushy-tailed and gooey-eyed, so I wouldn't be surprised if she was dating him. That doesn't mean I plan on calling her Mother Dearest any time soon.

"Each of you will return to your dorms immediately. You will also be joining me for detention tomorrow after your rep class." She claps her hands and herds the others in front. "Off with you now before I get the headmaster involved."

I slide Dracula a grin and then follow in their wake.

He steals a kiss in the common room before we're separated. A stupid big grin tilts my lips the entire way back to my room. Inside, Murie is nowhere to be seen, and I wonder if she's decided to sneak into Kal's room. It almost makes me wish I'd done the same with Dracula.

As I undress and get ready for bed, I think about Dracula and the party until a soft meow catches my attention. I walk over to the door and open it, startled to find a black cat looking up at me with its big yellow eyes.

"Oh, hey little kitty." The cat meows and then saunters past me. "Uhhh..." I just stand there looking at it for a moment. "Did Murie forget to tell me she's adopted a cat? Wouldn't be the first time she's done that," I say, closing the door with a soft click.

The cat hops up onto my bed and I climb up with her, holding out a hand for her to sniff. To my surprise, she bumps my hand and purrs before climbing up beside me. The silver medallion attached to her grey collar blinks in the light. I turn it around and read her name.

"Phantom?" I look down at the cat with a smile. "Are you a boy, Phantom?"

A quick peek under its belly tells me that he's very much a boy.

"Okay," I say, slipping under my cover and patting the pillow beside me. "You can sleep with me tonight. Just don't poop in my bed."

Phantom hisses and arches his back as though he understood what I said. I chuckle, stroking my hand down his back, and close my eyes.

CHAPTER NINE

*T*wo weeks after the party, things between Dracula and I are hotter than I could've imagined. When we aren't forced to attend Rep Classes, we hang out every chance we get, which usually involves us making out in hallways and closets, or just plain fooling around and getting to know each other.

It feels amazing to have a distraction at this academy. Dracula certainly takes my mind off the fact that I'm still stuck here for over two months. The way he looks at me like I'm the air to his lungs is utterly intoxicating. I never thought I'd find a boyfriend here, of all places. If I had known that, I would've turned that asshole's dick into stone a long time ago.

My relationship with Dracula isn't the only thing to blossom either. I've noticed how much time Murie's been spending with Kal, and while part of me misses hanging out with her, I'm relieved to see her happy like this.

As I make my way from the greenhouse, clutching my books to my chest, I can't help but smile at the thought of Murie's happiness and mine. Unfortunately, it's interrupted when Hades falls into step with me.

"I found one of the relics," he says, a dark grimace shadowing his features.

"Oh, cool. Where is it?" I ask, somewhat annoyed I didn't find it first, or at least be there with him when he did.

"I found it while you were fooling around with your new boyfriend."

I glare up at him, half wanting to laugh, the other wanting to lash out. What the hell is Hades' problem? I might mean something to him, but he doesn't mean jackshit to me, and yet he's acting like a jealous lover.

For the most part, I should be relieved that his jealousy has kept him out of my way. But there's something about the way he's acted over these past two weeks that bothers me. It shouldn't, but it does. It might have something to do with the fact he's been glaring holes into my skull whenever I've been with Dracula.

"I'll have you know I've been studying locations on the island," I say, scrunching my face at him, "but I haven't found anything so far. Where did you find this one?"

"I was... looking for something."

"Looking for something, huh?"

He shrugs, his gaze hardening. "A way off the island. I read this place used to connect the living realm to the dead, so I thought perhaps I could use the portal to get out of here. All I saw was the hammer but I couldn't reach it."

"Well, you still found it, so thank you." I slide through the door and follow him outside of the academy. "And if I happen to find any portals, I'll be sure to let you know. I want off this island just as much as you do."

Around ten minutes of strained silence later, we enter what I assume is the aforementioned field. Overgrown weeds flutter in the breeze and tickle my legs. Hades has already carved a path through them which leads us into an even greater poorly maintained field. With the paddocks, it looks more like a prairie than anything, but there are no animals around.

"It's just through here," Hades says, pointing to an arch in the trees opposite the field.

On the other side, we find a waterfall with a beautiful lagoon at the bottom. My bracelet comes alive, glowing and vibrating softly. He's right. One of the relics is close by.

"I had no idea this place was so close to the academy," I say, looking around the clearing.

"If you looked around once in a while you might actually..." He shakes his head, trailing off.

"I might actually what?" I probe him, cursing my curious nature. I shouldn't invite more conversation with him than necessary.

He waves a hand in dismissal. "Nothing." And then he points to the waterfall. "Can you swim?"

My feet root to the spot as my curiosity getting the

better of me. "Yeah. But first I want to know what you were going to say."

Hades shuts his eyes and takes in a deep, slow breath. After a few seconds, he exhales through his flared nostrils. "I was just going to say that if you didn't have tunnel vision, you'd find some pretty cool things on this island."

I tilt my head. "Tunnel vision? What the hell is that supposed to mean?"

"You know what it means, Zara."

Okay. Now he's starting to piss me off. Of course, I know what tunnel vision means, but I want to know in which context he's using it.

I cross my arms over my chest and squint my eyes at him, my hair rising statically. "Well?"

He stops to look at me, his thin blue eyebrows pulled together. "It means you're so focused on one thing that you're blind to all else going on around you."

"Well go on then, Sherlock. Tell me what I'm so focused on."

"Dracula."

"You're jealous," I say, a smirk curling my lips.

Hades' gaze darkens. "I am *not* jealous."

"Uh-huh. Then why are your hands clenched like that? And why have you been glaring at Drac for two weeks now? Yeah, I saw you."

Instead of providing an answer, he circles around me and walks to the edge of the lagoon. "Can we stay focused on the task at hand? Let's just get the damn thing and leave."

"Fine." I walk up alongside him and stare into the crystalline water. "Where's the relic?"

He points at the water bubbling ever so slightly in the middle of the lagoon. "It's right at the bottom, wedged between the rocks."

"Did it belong to Conquest? I mean, since it's a hammer and all."

He shakes his head, unbuttoning his shirt. "No. It belonged to War."

My gaze travels up his smooth, well-defined muscles, and dammit. Why does the guy who pisses me off more than anyone need to be fucking hot?

"How do you know the hammer is down there again?" I ask, removing most of my clothes but keeping my shirt and skirt on. Hades might be comfortable stripping down to his underwear, but I'm not.

"I was swimming when I saw it." He tosses his shirt to the ground. "I couldn't pull it out. I suppose that's why the headmaster said we need to do this together."

I nod, laying my belongings on a nearby rock. "Okay. I'll go first."

"We should swim down together," he says, walking to the side of the waterfall with me. "We'll probably reach the bottom faster if we dive from the top."

"Good idea."

I climb the rocks on the side of the waterfall with him until we're standing at the top. Although it's not a particularly big waterfall, it suddenly looks much bigger from up here. I peer over the edge and try to convince myself into jumping when Hades' voice catches me.

"I'm not the guy you think I am."

I turn to look at him, surprised by the quietness of his tone. "And what kind of guy is that?

He looks down at the water plunging into the lagoon. "Someone you detest."

"I don't detest you, Hades. You just... left a bad first impression on me."

I'm surprised by my own honesty.

His gaze flits over to meet mine, and for a moment he just looks at me. "I must have come across as crazy the first day we met."

"Crazy? You were practically calling me your soul-mate and declaring your love for me. I'd never even met you before. I thought you were a psychopath."

Silence stretches between us, with only the water-fall rushing in the background.

"You're right. I'm sorry for how we met. I was just..." He shakes his head again. "I wish I could change how I reacted that day."

"It's... alright," I say, not sure what else to add. I never expected Hades to be so open like this and he's coming across genuinely apologetic.

"It's not alright. I have a hard time with social inter-actions, however it's no excuse."

For some reason, that makes me smile. "I have noticed you interact a bit differently from the other guys I know."

That seems to compliment him. His eyes widen and he smiles, just slightly.

"Why do you struggle with social stuff?" I ask.

He hesitates momentarily. "I'm a bit of a loner. I

grew up in foster homes and pretty much kept to myself in hopes that whoever was going to adopt me wouldn't send me back like all the others. But it never worked. With the kind of adults I had in my life, social interaction wasn't really top of their to-do lists. Tons of arguments and disappointment, but not a lot of how to interact in a modern way."

"A modern way?" I repeat, frowning at him.

A shadow drifts over his face, darkening the more he stays quiet. I can't believe it, but the guy has actually got me feeling sorry for him. It couldn't have been easy living in foster care, especially when you're dumped with adults who couldn't give a shit about you. I was so lucky Seceila found me outside the temple, or who knows what would've happened to me. Hades didn't have that kind of luck.

"I'm sorry for what happened to you," I add quietly. "And do you know something? I'm not the girl you think I am, either. Maybe we both got off on the wrong foot."

His dark expression vanishes like the sun breaking out from the cloud. "Do you think we could start again? Fresh, I mean? I would like to prove to you that I'm not crazy."

I nod hesitantly, taken by the hopeful expression on Hades' face. "Let's just get these relics first and take it from there," I say, turning back to the lagoon. "Thank the gods I'm a natural-born swimmer. My mother is sea born."

Hades steps back and I follow him, the two of us getting ready to jump.

"Let's make a deal," Hades says, his focus still on the water. "Whoever gets the hammer first, wins. If I win, I get to take you on a date."

I just manage to resist the urge to roll my eyes. Should've seen that coming.

"And what happens if I win?" I ask.

He gives a hesitant shrug. "Whatever you want."

"Okay." I rub my hands together. "I'll think on it. But for now, let's do this!"

"There's just one more th—wait!"

Hades' voice vanishes as I leap off the waterfall. The wind whistles through my hair and I press my palms together, cutting through the water below effortlessly. Since I'm not a Sea Witch like Murie, it takes me a while to get my bearings, but soon I'm swimming toward the bubbles at the bottom of the lagoon. The bracelet on my wrist glows brighter than it has ever done, and I let it guide me to the hammer.

Just as I wrap my hand around the gold handle, a dark shape flickers in the corner of my eye. I keep my hand on the hammer but spin around, trying to see what it is. My hair floats around me and the water threatens to invade my senses. And then I catch sight of it.

A kelpie.

The sea creature whooshes past me, nothing but a mere blur. I've seen enough kelpies to know how vicious they are and fiercely protective of their treasure. Something tells me it doesn't want to give up the hammer. Its seaweed coat whips around it like a billowing cloak and I let out a surprised scream at the sheer size of it, instantly regretting it when I lose air.

Hades plunges into the water beside me, his hand covering mine on the hammer. Unfortunately, the kelpie comes charging back again, its hooves cutting through the water and kicking Hades to the side. Panic assails me and I let go of the relic, unable to avoid the kelpie when it shoves its head into my chest, knocking the last of the air out from my body.

Before I start to drown, I swim as fast as I can to the surface, taking in lungfuls of air when I can breathe again. I barely see the waterfall when the kelpie hits me with its nose and I'm thrust out of the lagoon and onto the grass. Tears sting my eyes as water invades my nose and I spit out as much water as I can. And then a hand hits me on the back, and I turn to see Hades holding the gilded hammer.

"You... you got it?" I barely manage to get the words out without choking again.

"Not by myself. You loosened it and I was able to pull it out." His eyes narrow as he removes his hand from my back. "I wish you didn't jump like that. I was trying to warn you about the guardian."

"The kelpie." My throat is still raw from all the coughing. "Yeah, I wish you warned me sooner."

He sits down on the grass beside me, his wet clothes hugging his body like a second skin. I glance down at my own clothes and a rush of heat rises to my cheeks at the sight of my breasts visible through my transparent shirt. I hold my arms over my chest.

"Why are we always falling into wet things?" I say.

To my surprise, Hades just laughs, and I find myself giggling with him.

"I do believe this means I won," he says once we've stopped laughing.

I let out an exaggerated sigh. Truthfully, I'm not as bothered about the whole date thing as I thought I'd be.

"Okay, a deal's a deal. Just tell me when and where."

Hades smiles like I've just walked up the aisle and told him 'I Do'. He stands and holds out his hand. "I'll pick you up on Sunday."

I take his hand, fighting the spark that shoots up my arm when he touches me.

"Just don't start calling me your love, or I swear to the gods, I will kill you and make it look like an accident," I warn, letting go of his hand.

He grins. "Alright, you've got yourself a deal. Now we just need to find the last two relics. I hope you know if I find them, it means two extra dates for me."

I stand on my tiptoes and pat him on the head. "Don't count on it, buddy, 'cause I'm winning next time."

Again he smiles, and it's ridiculously contagious.

CHAPTER TEN

I wrap my arms around my mother and hug her, breathing in her sea water scent.

"I've missed you, darling," she says, squeezing me before holding me at arm's length to assess me like she just did with Murie. "Have you been playing nice with the other poor creatures locked up in here?"

I wave a hand around the busy visitation room and roll my eyes. "Don't I always, Mum?"

She chuckles, the corner of her lips twitching. "Come and sit so I can hear all about your first month at the academy. I bet it's been just *riveting*."

My mother is definitely where Murie and I get our sarcastic sense of humor from.

Murie leads us to the only bench in the hall that isn't occupied. I pass Dracula on the way and smile at him, but he's too busy glaring at his father to notice me. At least I think it's his father; they look so alike.

His dad sits on a bench across from him, but he's looking over his head instead of at him. They are both dressed in black clothes, looking like they're at a funeral more than anything, and they wear the same ring on the same finger with the gleaming ruby stone.

I look around at the other visitors. Loki sits on his own by the barred window, scribbling away in a notebook. Hades is the only one I can't see as I join my family.

"Zara? Are you listening, dear?" My mother waves a hand in front of me.

Murie giggles from my side, but I do notice how she casts a glance at Kal from across the hall and blushes when he and an older woman wave at her.

"Huh?" I blink and shake my head. "Sorry, Mum. What did you say?"

"I was asking about your time here so far. Neither of you have used your... present I gave you."

I reach for my locket and gently brush my fingers over the primrose.

Murie does the same and the two of us smile sheepishly.

"We've just been busy," Murie says, glancing, once again, at Kal.

Mother follows her gaze and then nods. "Ah, I thought as much." She smiles warmly. "Boys are a great distraction. Which has caught *your* attention, Zara? The werewolf in the corner? Or perhaps the fae I saw outside the hall? He couldn't take his eyes off you."

"What? Who?" I squirm in my seat, unsure of who she's talking about.

My sister giggles. "Mom, Zara's set her sights on a more...red-blooded male."

I shoot her a mock glare, but my mother stares hard at me, so I know I have to confess to her. She always finds out who I'm dating anyway. Sometimes I'm convinced she has every fish in the sea spying for her.

"It's—"

"Don't tell me," she cuts in, holding up a finger, her gaze flitting around the room. "Is it perhaps the raven-haired vampire looking at you from across the room?"

I look on instinct, and yup, Dracula is looking right at me.

His father also gazes my way, but his eyes are narrowed into ruby shards. Slowly his lips peel back into a snarl, revealing the tips of his fangs.

"I will take that reaction as a yes. I can see why you would be attracted to Dracula's son. Or the Count himself, for that matter. They have a beautiful allure about them."

"Mother!" Murie practically squeaks the word out, her face turning scarlet.

Our mother purses her cherry lips. "Well, it is true. They are a very handsome and powerful family. One of the oldest to date."

I continue to drown my mother and Murie out while I scan the room further. In the time we've been talking, two men have joined Loki close by to us. I can't hear their conversation with my mother talking in my ear, but I can tell from Loki's grimace that it's not a pleasant one.

A blond, muscular guy sits beside Loki, nudging him with his shoulder and ruffling his hair with his paw-sized hand. An even bigger man sits across from them both, a black eye patch covering his left socket, and scratches his thick grey beard. He shakes his head as if disgusted by what Loki just said, and I wish I could hear what they're talking about.

I wish I could help cheer Loki up.

Both Dracula *and* Loki have daddy issues. I wonder what happened between them all? It's not just because I'm curious, but part of me wants to understand so I can help take some of their pain away.

I scan the room again, but Hades is nowhere to be seen. *Where is he? Does he not have anyone to visit him today?* After what he told me last week at the waterfall, I shouldn't be surprised. And I shouldn't feel as sorry for him as I do, but I can't help it. I fight down a strange urge to leave and seek him out. My emotions must be written all over my face because mother waves a hand in my face and snaps me back to attention again.

"I'm beginning to wonder about you, darling," she says.

Even Murie is looking at me, her eyebrows knitted together. "Seriously, what's going on with you?"

"N-nothing. You're right, I'm just distracted by boys.."

Thankfully, my mother just smiles at me. "I remember those days with your father—Poseidon, rest his soul. He was such a handsome young man, I could hardly keep my eyes off him. Did you know I saved him from drowning? Yes, that's how we met. It feels like eons ago now." She shakes her head, her silver hair swaying behind her. I've heard the story of how she met her husband, and I will never tire of it. "Anyway, enough about me. How are you both doing here?"

It's Murie who answers first. "It's not as awful as Zara made out." She slides me a grin which I return. "It has its ups and downs, but we're holding in there."

I nod. "Yeah, it's not the prison I thought it was cracked up to be. Now we're just trying to enjoy the ride."

Murie snorts in laughter and I nudge her with my elbow.

Our mother looks between us, a thin brow raised. "I see."

"I didn't mean it like that," I say quickly, but Murie is still laughing her head off.

"Now, I may have left this a little bit late," my mother says, leaning over and placing a hand on each of our knees, "but when a man and women love each other—"

"Don't you dare," I growl, making Murie laugh even harder. "We already know."

Mother just laughs and leans back in her seat. "So long as you're safe. And please be careful with whom you get involved with here."

She looks away and I follow her gaze, weirdly already sensing who's looking at me.

Dracula and the Count are looking our way again. They might have overheard what we were saying because Dracula is stifling a grin while his father stares at me with that impassive look of his. Now it's my turn to blush as I look back at my mother.

"I have some other news," I say, trying to change the subject.

"Oh?" She perks up in her seat.

Murie tenses at my side. "Zara, maybe another ti—"

All the mirth vanishes from our mother's face and she becomes deadly serious as she glances at me. "Tell me what you were going to say, dear."

I take a deep inhale, a little unsure how to word it. "Well, on my first day here, I met the headmaster. His name is Eryc Knightford..." I trail off, swallowing a lump in my throat I didn't expect to feel. Maybe this isn't the best place to tell her.

Her hand falls on my knee again and she smiles softly at me. "Go on. You can tell me anything."

"He said that he's my biological dad."

The blood drains from my mother's face. For just a second, her composure breaks and panic seeps through the cracks, but then she clears her throat and nods.

"That's great news, darling."

I pause, watching her. She seems to be taking it okay, and I've been dying to tell her since we found out. I just didn't want to risk using my necklace to contact her.

"He knew all about you," I tell her, lowering my voice, "and about how you found me and where. He even had a picture of my birth mother."

"I'm so happy for you. This is very unexpected."

"And that's not it," Murie says, glancing at me. "He's also sent her on a quest to uncover some relics."

"A quest... to uncover... relics?" Mother repeats slowly. "What for?"

"To protect the school, apparently." Murie looks at me. "Right?"

"Right." I nod, shaking my foot a little nervously; I don't want to worry Seceila. "I found one on accident with a student named Hades. Mr Knightford said there's four in total buried across the island. He's asked us to work together to find them."

"I see." Mother slaps her lips together, her nostrils flaring as she breathes in. "Have you found any more?"

"Just one other," I say, still shaking my foot. "We have two left."

"Please be careful, dear."

My stomach clenches at the concern in her gaze. "I will. It's perfectly safe."

She eyes me for a moment, as if knowing that I'm lying to her. "I will be keeping a closer eye on you through the necklace." Tears well into her eyes and her voice breaks as she looks down at the purse in her lap.

"Mom, what's the matter?" Murie asks, moving to sit beside her.

I do the same while asking quietly, "If you're happy for me, why are you crying?"

It takes a moment for her to answer. She retrieves a handkerchief from her pocket and wipes her eyes first. "I'm worried that you won't need me anymore, darling"

"*What!*" both Murie and I shout at the same time, dragging unwanted attention from across the hall.

"What are you talking about?" I ask quietly.

"Now that you found your real father, you won't need me anymore." She dries her eyes again and then blows into the handkerchief. "I should not get emotional like this. It's not like I didn't know this day would happen. I knew the moment I held you in my arms outside the Forbidden Temple that one day you'd find your birth parents and leave."

"Mom…" I reach out and take her hand in mine. "That's ridiculous. I will *never* leave you. *You're* my mother. Nothing and no one can change or replace that. I love you."

I get up and wrap my arms around her in a tight, reassuring embrace. After a moment, I let go and wipe the tears from my own eyes, noticing Loki and his family are having a fairly heated conversation. I can hear them now that it's quiet and I don't like what little of their conversation I pick up.

"Try not to drown anyone this year," the blonde snarls at him, rising from the bench. "If you can manage, that is."

I furrow my brow. What the fuck?

'Try not to drown anyone this year'. What the hell is that supposed to mean?

My heart freezes at the pained expression on Loki's face. He stands, too, along with his father who couldn't look more disgusted to be with Loki if he tried. Loki catches me looking and flushes from his neck up. His gaze hardens as he snaps his attention back to his family.

"Don't bother visiting next month," he all but growls before storming out, leaving the guys standing looking a little shell-shocked.

A bell rings in the background, signalling that visitation is now over. I keep my gaze on the door where Loki stormed out.

"Time flew past too swiftly," Mother says, standing to hug us.

I squeeze her in my arms, and she returns it while exhaling a sigh of relief.

"You will always be my mum," I say firmly, and she kisses me on the cheek before leaving with the others. I'm sad to see her go.

Dracula marches past, knocking the table beside me, and marches out of the other door across the room, his hands balled into fists. I look to where Loki disappeared and then back at Dracula, wondering who to go see first. They both need someone right now, and I wish I could be in two places at once, but I can't.

CHAPTER ELEVEN

I pick up my pace as I run on the balls of my feet out of the courtyard, through the main halls, and into the forest. I see the back of Loki's head and run for him. He's going to the lake. My steps slow as I watch Loki pick a rock off the ground and skim it across the surface of the water. I don't think he's caught on that I'm here yet, so I keep myself hidden in the shadows of the trees, watching him.

Water laps at his feet as he sets his shoes on the ground beside him. The setting sun bathes him in amber hues while he picks up a pebble and throws it across the water. After a few skips, the stone sinks into the water, leaving a ripple in its wake.

He grabs another and attempts to skip it. The pebble jumps once and stops. He picks up a third, then a fourth, and gains a little more distance with each one. When he turns my way, his expression is determined, his brows pulled together in contemplation.

I smile to myself. I've never seen this side to him. He

almost looks a little vulnerable in a way. I step out of the trees and approach him.

"What are you doing here?" he asks, noticing me without lifting his head. He continues to skip pebbles across the lake, each one growing more momentum than the last.

"I could ask you the same thing," I say quietly, kicking my shoes off. My feet sink into the soft grass as I tiptoe over to him.

He pauses, then picks up another stone. "Do you know how to skip rocks?"

I take this as an invitation to stay and sit down on the grass with him, crossing my legs over each other. "No, actually."

He tosses another pebble into the lake; this one skips at least four times. "That's surprising."

"Why is it surprising?"

"Isn't your mother from the sea?"

I blink at him, surprised he knows this about me. He's clearly been doing a little research.

"She is," I say, picking up a flat stone and running my fingers over the smooth surface. "But why would that mean I know how to skip rocks?"

He shrugs, throwing another stone that skips five times. Now he's making me want to try it. "It wouldn't," he says. "It would just mean you're around water a lot as a kid. Kids get bored. Kids who get bored around water tend to do one of three things: swim in it, throw stuff in it, learn to skip rocks." He skips another and it jumped five times before sinking.

I nod, impressed. "Maybe you could teach me then."

He smiles and looks at me from the side of his eye. "It's not something that can be taught in a few minutes."

"I've got more than a few minutes," I tell him, shielding my gaze from the blinding sunray that captures his features. "Why are you out here, Loki?"

The muscles in his face clench hard. "I needed some time alone."

I bite the inside of my mouth, wondering if I should probe to get him to open up. He didn't refuse to answer me, so maybe he does want to talk about what happened in the visitation hall.

"Is it about what your family said to you?"

His green eyes widen as the blood drains from his pale face. "You heard that."

It's not a question, but I nod anyway. "Everyone in the hall did."

"Yeah." He nods, clenching a rock in his hand until his knuckles turn white. "Figured they did. My brother Thor enjoys mocking me, especially when there are people around. He's been like that since our mother was slain at the hands of the Frost Giants back on our planet. That's why he changed. He blamed me for her death since my biological father was a giant."

For a long while, he's silent while he tosses more rocks into the lake. The sun warms my skin and I savor it as I watch him. The tension in his shoulders lessens the more he skips rocks.

"Why are you at the academy?" I ask him softly.

He pauses, only briefly, before dropping an

unwanted rock onto the ground. "Didn't you hear Captain Nemo on the ship?"

I nod. "He said you tried to take over Asgard again. The rumors say that too."

"Rumor?" He grins at me. "That's the first I've ever heard it referred to like that."

"Isn't that what it is? A rumor?"

"You don't think it's the truth?" He seems surprised by this.

I shake my head. "No, I don't."

He sits back and studies me. "Interesting. And why is that, I wonder?"

"It just doesn't feel right to me," I say, shrugging. "The rumor also doesn't add up when I look at you. I think deep down, you're much sweeter than you make out, and I don't think you'd try to take over your planet."

Loki's eyes flash and darken when he looks at me. "And what if I told you it wasn't a rumor? That I did try to take over Asgard, more than once?"

I bite my lower lip before answering. "Who am I to judge anyone? I got sent here because I turned a guy's dick into st—"

"Stone and then wore it as a necklace," he interjects, smirking at me. "I remember."

We chuckle quietly, then train our gaze on the sun slipping toward the auburn horizon.

"The real reason I'm here?" His voice is just above a whisper. "Part of it is because of Thor. He's my brother by name, but not by blood. When he found out we weren't related, he changed. We were just kids at the time, but he changed. Life's been hell ever since. I couldn't take it anymore—the ridicule, constantly living in his shadow, never matching up to my parents' expectations." His eyes close for a second. "I just wanted it all to end."

I reach out and gently place my hand over his on the grass. "I'm sorry they put you through that."

His eyes open, and his expression softens at my touch. "Thank you." Then he looks back at the horizon and throws another stone in. "The other reason is that I wanted to get revenge on that asshole."

My stomach clenches as images of Dracula and Loki fighting in the cafeteria fill my head. "What asshole?" I ask quietly.

Loki's gaze locks on me, darkening. "Dracula. The one you've been seeing. I'll never understand what you see in a murderer like him."

When he pulls his hand back and fixes his attention on the sunset, I fall quiet, unable to think of a reply. I know he has history with Dracula and I'm not sure I'll ever be able to mend it, but I am curious to hear from Loki's point of view.

"What did Drac do to you?"

His jaw clenches as a light breeze lifts his raven hair over his shoulders. "He's the reason my sister is gone. I hate that fucking bloodsucker and I hate that you and so many others don't see him for the monster he is!" I wince at the sudden increase in his voice, and Loki glances at me. The anger in his gaze is replaced with sheer and utter pain. "He's the one who killed her, Zara, not me. My family has never forgiven me for Alena's loss, and I don't deserve their forgiveness, but I will *never* take the blame for her death. I loved my sister... I loved her!"

I reach out once more, relieved when he doesn't reject me when I touch his shoulder. He pulls his knees up and loops his arms around them.

"Sorry," he says after a moment. "I didn't mean to lash out."

"You weren't lashing out. And I'm the one who asked."

His lips twitch. "True. You are an inquisitive girl."

"That's a nice way to put it," I counter dryly.

He smiles and shrugs his shoulder, nudging my hand playfully.

"I like this side of you, Loki."

"What? Vengeful?"

"No." I scoot closer to him so that my feet touch the water. "Vulnerable. It makes you more… relatable. But I will say one thing."

He arches an eyebrow at me. "Oh, yeah?"

I lean in, bringing my lips to his ear. "If you hurt Drac, I will turn your precious manhood into stone and add it to my trophy collection. I am *not* kidding."

His shoulders tense under my grasp, and then he laughs. "You really like him, don't you?" he asks once he's composed himself.

"I do. Please promise you won't hurt him? You can dislike him, but please... for me... for your own sanity... don't let your hatred for him turn you into a monster. Only you can let it do that, and when it comes down to it, it's just not worth it."

For a long while, he just studies me, and I hold his gaze, silently imploring him.

"I can't promise I will never hurt him," he says, "but I will promise not to hurt him so long as he doesn't hurt you. Then the deal's off, and I *will* kill him."

I release a breath I wasn't even aware I had been holding. I'm not sure if Loki is being honest or just telling me what I want to hear, but I really hope it's the former. And the way he promises to kill Dracula if he hurts me... Of course, I won't let that happen—ever—but it makes me all hot inside.

"Thank you, Loki."

Now he's smirking at me, his forlorn expression all but gone. He opens his mouth as if he's about to speak, but then he leans forward and covers my lips with his. I hesitate at first, slightly taken by surprise, before I open up and reciprocate the kiss.

Loki's lips are soft and warm, and when his hand falls to my waist and gently caresses me, a rush of desire shudders down the length of my spine. I reach out and thread my hand in his long hair. The tresses are like silk between my fingers. I moan into his mouth, loving the peppermint taste of him.

"Fuck, I've wanted to do that since I saw you on the boat," he says once we part for air.

Heat rises into my cheeks, staining them the same color as my hair. "Me too."

He grins at that and then rises to his feet, offering me his hand. "Come, my lady. It's time you learned the art of stone skipping. And perhaps you can tell me where you've been sneaking off to all the time"

I chuckle and take his hand. Skipping stones and telling Loki about the Gilded Four is not how I imagined I'd spend my evening, but I couldn't be happier. Now if I could just keep my guys from killing each other...

CHAPTER TWELVE

*L*oki looks around before he steals a kiss. I jokingly hit his chest and pull back, glancing around the castle entrance. Nobody is paying us any attention, but I'd still prefer if we kept whatever the hell is going on between us private. At least until I tell Dracula. I don't want him to find out from someone else that I'm kissing his sworn enemy. Hopefully, when I'm not kissing them, I can help mend the bridges that were burned in the wake of Alena's death; I still don't quite know what happened, but I plan on finding out.

I part ways with Loki outside the main hall and watch him glance over his shoulder at me when I look back at him. A grin slides over my lips as I climb the grand stairs toward Mr Knightford's office. I barely step into the hallway leading to it when I hear my mother's voice.

"How *dare* you do this to me!"

Her bellow is so unlike her that I momentarily

root to the spot, stunned by the venom lacing her words. Slowly, I creep down the hall and linger by the door, my heart racing. I know I shouldn't be eavesdropping. But why is my mother shouting at the headmaster, my biological father? Dread churns my stomach. I should've known she would be upset over the news.

You're such an idiot, Zara!

The sound of something smashing on the floor causes me to flinch and hold my breath. It's followed by a gasp of air, and it takes me a second to realize someone is being choked. That alone has me throwing open the door and marching inside.

The person choking is Mr Knightford.

My mother holds him up in the air, her tentacles wrapped around him like a vise.

"Mom, stop!" I scream, running over to her.

Her head snaps toward me and panic blossoms over her face. "D-Darling. I was just..." She looks back at the headmaster's purpling face and lets him go. "...talking to your birth father."

Mr Knightford falls to the floor, his mask falling off his face. I hurry over to him and help him up. When he snatches his mask from me and tries to cover his face, I catch sight of the scars embedded deep within his flesh and around his eye socket.

"How can he talk to you if you're strangling him?" I snap, a sudden protectiveness surging through me. "Mom, you were choking him!"

Reality dawns on her, and the color drains from her face. Her tentacles vanish underneath her dress and she takes a step back, almost like she's startled by what she nearly did.

"Sir, are you okay?" I turn to the headmaster, but he just waves a hand in dismissal.

"I am. Your... your mother can be quite intimidating. I see where you get it from."

I frown, surprised by his comment. "You think I'm intimidating?"

"No, not to me." He dusts his robes and smiles at me. "But to the other students, perhaps. Assertive is the appropriate term and I find it useful to have."

My mother steps forward, her hand reaching out to me. "Zara, dear, I was just making sure he's going to protect you." She slides him a hard glare, and he holds it unwaveringly.

"Of course I will protect her. She is my daughter," Mr Knightford spits back, his hands balling into fists by his side. "I have been giving her time to adjust to the academy and the fact that I'm her real father. That does not mean I haven't been protecting her."

At that exact moment, Phantom jumps up from behind the desk and meows at me. Mr Knightford turns to him and scratches his chin. And here I had assumed Murie adopted another stray cat.

"If you are protecting my daughter, then what is this I hear of quests and relics? Zara is supposed to be protected while at this academy. Not forced to do your dirty work for you," my mother hisses at him.

"Mom, it's okay." I step between them, more to prevent her from attacking him again. Seceila has always been overprotective, especially after Murie's dad died, so I should've known this would happen. "I'm a grown adult and I want to help Mr Knightford. Besides, I've already found two of them and it's... fun, looking for them."

I refrain from telling her that I almost drowned because I'm certain she'll throttle the headmaster with all six of her tentacles.

My mother cups my face with her hands, her silver lashes flecked with tears. "I just want you to be safe, darling. I'm sorry for hurting—"

"Nearly killing," I counter with an arched brow.

She nods. "Nearly killing your headmaster. I just worry about you. I promised your father I would never let anything bad happen to you. The fact that you are in this... place... is confirmation that I have failed. Now to be told you are running around the island in search of relics that could potentially harm you...?" She shakes her head, and I gently squeeze her hand.

"I promise you I'm not in any danger. You know I have a way of contacting you if I am," I say, referring to the primrose tucked under my shirt.

My mother nods before pressing a kiss to my forehead. "I love you, my sweet daughter."

"And I love you, too, Mom."

Phantom meows, breaking up the tender moment. My mother kisses me four times on the forehead before she leaves the room; she gives Mr Knightford a warning glare before doing so.

I turn to him, asking quietly, "What was all that really about?"

He picks Phantom up into his arms and walks

around his desk, settling in his high-backed chair. "I do not blame your mother for wishing to protect you. For eighteen years I have mourned the inability to do so. It's perfectly understandable that she wishes to keep you out of harm's way. I imagine she was surprised at being told I was your biological father during your first visitation." He lifts one eyebrow at me, and I try not to squirm under his perusal. "In time, I believe she will trust me, and that's all that matters."

He motions me to sit in the chair opposite him, which I do slowly, looking at the way Phantom dotes on him.

"Your cat's been sleeping with me most nights," I say, nodding at him.

Mr Knightford nods and strokes the cat's head. "Yes, I asked Phantom to keep an eye on you. He's grown terribly fond of you, Zara."

I smile. "He does help me fall asleep when he purrs like that."

The headmaster chuckles. "And it is rare for him to purr. He knows a good heart when he sees one." He looks up at me, his expression sobering a little. "I have some good news regarding the relics."

"You do?"

I watch him open his desk drawer and pull out a leather tome with gold handwriting.

"Mrs Morgana found this in her archive yesterday evening. Most of the text is an ancient tongue long forgotten, but I wonder if there will be clues to where the other relics are located once translated." Again he reaches into the drawer and pulls out another heavy-looking book. "This will help you translate the clues."

He slides the books over and I pick them up, hugging them to my chest. "This is perfect. Truthfully, we were a little stuck on where to look for the other two."

"I'm glad I could help." His eyes narrow on me for just a second. "Mr Erebus informed me today that you are going on a date with his son Hades. Is that correct?"

My heart clenches in my chest and heat rises to my cheeks. "Umm... I may have agreed to go on a date with him if he found the relic first."

Mr Knightford holds up a hand. "No need to explain. I technically have no right to ask this of you, but please, Zara, be careful. Hades is not the kind of boy I would suggest you associate yourself with. In fact, I would suggest none of the boys at this academy. They are not here for minor offences."

"I'm not here for a minor one either," I remind him, my pulse spiking. "And I don't think the people here are as awful as you think."

He watches me for a long, tense moment. "Perhaps there is some truth in that. My aim is that by the time the students leave my academy, they will have learned from their sins and can start their lives anew. Right now, their paths are crooked, so I only wish you to be cautious of this. Will you?"

I clench the books tighter to my chest. "Yes, of course."

Mr Knightford exhales deeply. "Thank you. Now, where is this date taking place?"

"I'm not really sure. He just said he'd pick me up tomorrow."

Phantom hops off Mr Knightford's lap and walks over the desk toward me. "It appears Phantom would like to accompany you," he says to me. "He is fiercely protective of those he imprints on. Will you take him with you?"

After a pause, I nod and stand from the chair. Phantom jumps onto the floor and stands beside me.

"Very good." Mr Knightford smiles, though it doesn't quite reach his eyes. "Good luck on your date, Zara."

"Thanks. And thank you for the book. I think it'll help find the last two relics."

He smiles at me. "I do hope so."

With Phantom at my side, I leave Mr Knightford's office while flipping through the heaviest book. So far I can't see anything about the sword, but I do find a small passage about the bow. At least I think it's the bow based on the diagram. Before I know it, I reach my dorm room. I strip into my floral pyjamas, curl up on the bed with Phantom and a cup of hot liquorice tea, and I read the books until sleep eventually takes me.

CHAPTER THIRTEEN

I can't believe I'm about to go on a date with Hades.

Clipping the last of my pink curls into place, I stand back and look at my reflection in the bathroom mirror. The dark green dress with the sweetheart neckline hugs my curves perfectly. It also matches the necklace my mother gave me, accentuating the emerald jewel in the middle. I still haven't used the primrose in the weeks I've been here, but I doubt that will be for long. I guess I've just been so preoccupied with boys and finding sacred relics, which is a good thing since I'm trapped at this academy against my will.

My gaze strays to the other necklace resting in the valley of my throat. The primrose. It's all I have of my parents. I wonder if Mr Knightford would recognise it?

I slip my feet into my small heels and nod. This is as good as I get.

Just as I'm about to turn away and leave, a loose strand of hair falls away and turns into a snake.

"Oi, stop it, you!" I giggle as I wrestle her back into the clip.

"Who are you talking to?" Murie asks, stepping into the room with two pizza boxes.

"My hair."

"Girl, you're crazy. But that's why I love you." She grins as she walks over to her bed and dumps the boxes down. "Isn't it funny how we both have dates tonight?"

I cast a longing glance at her pizza. "I'm a little envious of yours."

She sits cross-legged on her bed and tilts her head at me. "Where is Hades taking you again?"

"He didn't say. And don't worry, I'll be careful."

My sister breathes out a sigh of relief. "Good. I mean, he seems perfectly harmless, if not slightly infatuated with you, but you can never be too careful."

I pause in the mirror, my fingers still adjusting my hair while Mr Knightford's warning plays through my head.

"I'll be careful," I repeat, more to myself than anything.

"And have fun," she practically sing-songs as I pull my backpack on and leave our room with a grin.

Hades is waiting for me outside, right on time. The sleeves of black shirt are rolled up to the elbow, displaying just hints of a tattoo around his left elbow. His skinny jeans sculpt him tightly and his blue hair is slicked back with only a few loose strands falling into his amber eyes. He smiles upon seeing me.

"Wow." His gaze roves slowly over the length of my body. "You look breathtaking."

"Thank you," I say, my cheeks heating up as I give him a slow once over. "You don't look too shabby yourself."

He grins at that and holds out his arm. "Shall we?"

Nervously, I accept, and he leads me out of the academy. The afternoon sun is high in the clear-blue sky and I take in a deep breath of the fragrant air.

"So, where are we going?" I ask, but Hades just shrugs.

"It's a surprise."

I eye him closely. Surprises aren't really my thing, but I let him have his moment. I decide to tell him about the book Mr Knightford gave me and that I've got a lead on at least one of the relics.

"I found out that the bow is from the Horseman, Conquest," I tell him. "Most of the text here is written in ancient Greek, but I've managed to translate some of it."

"Oh?" He side-glances me. "I didn't know you could speak Greek."

"Just a little. It's strange because I don't remember studying it in school. Anyway, the bow is said to be buried inside the oldest tree on the island. I just don't know where that is."

"Well, I can also speak the language, so I'll help you translate. We'll figure it out together." He falls quiet and bites his lip in contemplation. "Is there anything about the last relic?"

"Famine's sword?" I shake my head. "Not yet. But I'll keep translating as much as I can."

I look around the field he's taken me to, surprised

by how far from the academy we've walked. The flowers swaying in the light breeze are almost the same blue as his hair, but the petals are mixed with streaks of white. I bend down to pluck one of them and it feels like silk.

"I love spring," I whisper, closing my eyes as I inhale the flower's scent.

It smells like the candy, parma violets.

When I open my eyes again, Hades has plucked a handful of flowers and waves his hand over them. He holds the bracelet out to me. My heart stutters in my chest, flaring with a desire I never thought I'd feel for Hades.

"Thank you," I say, pulling the bracelet onto my wrist with the snake. "Is this where our date is?"

"Just a little further." He nods to the cluster of trees bathed in sunlight.

Curiously I follow him through them and I'm taken aback by the stunning fountain shooting a stream of water into the air. I let go of Hades' arm and peer into the fountain. Gold coins shimmer beneath the surface, reflecting the light.

"Wow," is all I can say, transfixed by the fountain's beauty.

Hades beams at me. "I thought you might like this one."

"I do. How the hell do you keep finding all these cool spots?"

He walks over to the fountain and peers down at the coins. "I've spent a lot of time on this island. This is by far my favorite place. Do you like it?"

"Like it? I love it." I frown at him, a mischievous grin pulling at my lips. "Did Murie tell you that I love wishing wells?"

"No, no. I wasn't aware 'til now." I watch him run his fingers over the smooth stone, a look of contentment on his face. "This fountain isn't like the others. It's magical. Sacred."

"What makes it magical and sacred?" I ask, peering again into the fountain. The water is so clear that I can see my reflection on the coins.

"It has restorative purposes."

I glance at him. "Like the Fountain of Youth?"

"Not quite, but it is carved from the same stone." He swipes a hand through the water and it trickles like sand between his fingers. "This one restores memories and past lives that were once lost." Reaching into his suit pocket, he retrieves two gold coins and tosses one at me, which I manage to catch. "Throw it in, Zara. Make a wish."

My breath hitches as I look down at the coin, the fountain, and then at him. Everything has suddenly gotten super tense between us.

"What kind of wish?" I ask softly.

His expression is almost hopeful. "I'm hoping you'll wish to remember me."

I take a step back, clutching the coin in my hand like a talisman. Instead of being afraid of Hades and his imagined life with me, I'm intrigued. A need to under-stand him burns deep within me. This wish needs to work.

His hand rests over mine and he looks deeply into

my eyes. "Please, Per... Zara. Make the wish. I beg of you."

From his tone and expression alone, I'm unable to refuse him.

I close my eyes, hold my breath, and toss the coin into the fountain while thinking perhaps there is a morsel of truth behind Hades' words. The coin splashes into the water and I wait several moments before opening my eyes again.

Hades steps forward, his hands outstretching, but he halts with the clear realization that I have not remembered whatever he hoped I would.

"I'm still the same," I say quietly, my chest tightening.

He closes his eyes, a crease etched between his brows. "I know."

"Sorry it didn't go as you planned."

Now he looks at me, a hint of a smile teasing his lips. "No matter. I wanted to show you this fountain, anyway."

I smile back at him. "I'm glad you did. Now it's your turn to make a wish."

He turns toward the fountain and gazes into the water for a moment. I'm almost tempted to ask him what he's going to wish for, but something tells me it's about my supposed lost memories. I wish I knew what he was talking about. If what he's saying is true and he knew me in a past life, I don't recall him and I'm not sure I ever will.

For once, I feel sorry for him. To have no family or friends, and then the girl you're apparently in love with doesn't remember you... Yeah, that'd suck pretty hard.

Once Hades tosses his coin into the water, he sits down on the edge of the fountain. "I'm sorry this date didn't work out like I planned."

I sit beside him, closer than I expected. "It's been fun."

He looks at me, hopeful. "Really?"

"Yeah. And hey, we didn't get wet this time," I say, making Hades laugh.

"I've longed to spend this time with you," he whispers, gazing deeply into my eyes. The intense way he looks at me has my breath catching in my throat. "I hope with time you'll be able be to remem—"

He stops, suddenly wrapping an arm around his chest.

"What's wrong?" I ask, scanning him for any signs of injury.

"N-nothing." He sucks a deep breath in through his nose, his lips pressing into a line. "Just a bit of pain."

He's acted this way before, but from the way his face is contorted in anguish, the pain is getting worse; so much that he can no longer hide it.

"I think we should go back and get you to the infirmary," I say, standing from the fountain.

He stands with me, albeit a little unsteadily. "I am perfectly fine. Please don't worry about it."

I cross my arms and bite the inside of my mouth. He doesn't look perfectly fine. However, he clearly doesn't want my help or me to keep talking about it. I don't know why, but the sight of him in pain doesn't bring me the satisfaction I wanted the first day I met him.

"Come on," he says, nodding toward the trees. "I'll walk you back."

Something tells me he *really* doesn't want me to know what's wrong with him.

"I had a nice time with you," I say, falling into step with him. "You're not as loco as I thought you were."

His arm slackens around his stomach as he flashes me a smile. "Then my mission has been accomplished."

Later that night, I dream about Hades and the fountain. However, this time the blue flowers have wilted, and the fountain is filled with pomegranates instead of coins. I lean forward and scoop one of the pomegranates out. The second I touch it, the fruit rots in my hand, and Hades' voice cuts through the trees shrouded in the darkness around me.

"Persephone! Persephone, come back to me!"

CHAPTER FOURTEEN

Mr Blackbird slams the door behind him and marches to the front of the classroom. He's the one professor everyone hates with a passion. On the first day I had his Rep Four class, he made us copy textbooks for over two hours, and it's pretty much been the same ever since. Sometimes he throws a lecture in, but generally his main focus appears to be boring us to death. He reminds me of my former headmaster back in Atlantis and I hated him, too.

I look up from my notebook and narrow my eyes on him. He paces in front of his desk, his dusty black robes whipping behind him, and taps his metal rod against the chalkboard. He usually holds it like a whip while his sharp blue eyes scan everyone like shards of ice.

If it wasn't for the awful affectations he's adopted on a daily basis, he might just be attractive. It doesn't help that the class itself is boring. Nothing but reading the textbook and learning about what happens to villains who do not atone during their time here. Maybe that's why he puts on the threatening disposition: to remind us who and where we are. I'm not sure if it actually works because, for me, his class just makes me tired. I yawn and Murie nudges me in the ribs before Mr Blackbird catches it and singles me out to the class.

"Oh, I'm sorry, Miss Zara. Am I boring you?"

The whole class turns to look at me in unison.

"Busted," Murie mutters under her breath.

I manage to swallow the rest of my yawn and straighten in my chair, my cheeks stained pink. "No, Mr Blackbird, not at all."

"Then repeat what I just said to the class." He pivots so quickly that his blond hair takes a moment to settle back in place. "Come on. I don't have all day."

Murie's eyes go wide, conveying my doom. Shit.

"With pleasure," I say, the faintest hint of sarcasm lacing my words.

Little does Mr Blackbird know that I have long mastered the art of listening, even when I appear as though I'm not. I hold my notebook and recite what he just said about villains and atonement.

Mr Blackbird slaps his lips together. "Very good," he says after a moment, then continues with the lecture. Shortly after, the bell rings, and I shove my books into my bag and pull the straps over my shoulders.

"What are you doing right now?" I ask Murie as we retreat out of the hall.

"Nothing, you?"

"Nothing. Want to hang out?"

My sister's face lights up like sunbeams. "I'd freaking love to!"

She links her arm with mine as we make our way out of the academy and into a clearing I've never seen before. I glance at the sun sliding behind the edge of the island before resting my head on her shoulder. Pollen and dandelion wisps flutter around us as we sit down on a fallen tree.

"I've missed this," I say, closing my eyes and basking in the warmth of the sun against my skin.

"Me too."

"I feel like we haven't hung out much since we got here."

Murie laughs, her shoulder shaking my head. "That's because we haven't."

"We've both been spending too much time with boys," I add, opening my lids to peek at her.

"Is it too much, though?" She gives me a grin followed by a wink.

I grin at her. "I suppose not, but I do miss you."

My sister smiles and kisses me on the head. "I miss you too, Zee. But speaking of boys…" She straightens on the trunk and turns to look at me. "Kal and I think we figured out the portrait of Dorian Gray. Remember? From our first day here?"

I nod. "I do remember. You guys actually figured it out?"

I've admittedly been too focused on the relics to research about the portrait.

"We think so," she says, nodding. "We'll present our

idea to her next time we're in class and see what Miss Morgana says."

"That's great news!"

"Yeah, and get this… We also found this lost trident he's been looking for forever."

I lift my head to look at her. "Lost trident?"

She waves a hand dismissively. "It's a long story, but basically, there was a curse placed on his mom and that's the reason he's here. He wants to help her. I felt bad for him, so we've been spending a lot of time looking for the trident. We finally found it just the other day."

"Ah, so that's where you've been all these nights." I slide her a grin. "I just figured you two were always doin' it."

Murie gives a horrified shriek and smacks me on the arm with a laugh. "Not always. But I am really into him."

"Uh-huh. I can tell."

"Alright, well, what about you? You and Hades were also hunting for relics, weren't you? And you had that date with Dracula."

"And a thing with Loki," I add quietly.

"*What?* Loki, too?" Murie lifts a hand to her mouth in mock disbelief. "Oh, Zara, you have been busy!"

I shove her playfully. "Shhh! Shut up!"

She giggles. "Damn, girl. I'm a little envious."

I wave her off. "At any rate, I've been more interested in finding these last two relics with Hades. Mr Knightford gave me a book with some clues."

"What are they?" she asks, watching me shrug my backpack off and rummage through the contents.

I pull the books out and show them to her. "There's a bow and a sword. I'm not sure where the sword is, but the bow is supposed to be carved into or from the oldest tree on the island. Something like that. I'm not sure. The wording in the book is kind of tricky, and I need to use the other book to translate it."

She scans the two of them, her eyebrows furrowing. "Is this written in Greek?"

I nod. "Yup. My strange ability to speak some of it has finally come in use."

"Hmm." She continues flipping through the books. "Have you gotten any closer to finding them?"

"Not yet, but Hades is helping with the translations. He can speak Greek, too."

She lifts her gaze up from the books. "Okay, back to boy talk. Who are you most interested in?"

I scrunch my face. "Can't I have all of them?"

Murie lifts up her hands. "Hey, I ain't one to judge. You do you, girl, so long as you don't hurt anyone."

I grin up at her. "Now *that* I can't promise... Hades can really push my buttons sometimes." My gaze drifts to the flower bracelet on my wrist. "But I like him. He's not the crazy asshole I thought he was."

"Liking him is a good start," she says, standing with the books balanced in her arms. "Maybe try not to throw him into the lake again."

"Don't worry. We seem to be getting wet without me doing that."

My sister stares at me like I've just grown another head. "What?"

"Oh my gosh, not like that!" I hurriedly get to my feet and take the books from her, distracting myself with shoving them back into my bag. "I just mean, we fell into Ms Athame's cauldron and then a waterfall a few days ago."

"Mhm." If Murie wants to say anything else about it, she doesn't.

Which is good because my face is on fire.

As we walk through the forest back toward the academy, the bracelet on my wrist comes to life again with a soft glow and hiss.

"Oh, my sweet fuck. Murie, look!" I smack her on the arm several times. "Look, look, look, look, look!"

"Jeez, will you quit with the hitting!" She rubs her arm and glares at me before following my gaze. "What am I supposed to be looking at?"

"This." I hold my bracelet up for her to see. "When it glows, it means there's a relic nearby. Come on, we need to hurry!"

The pull of the magic guides me through the towering trees. My footfalls are swift and heavy as I look around in search of the relic. With all the towering trees, it must be the bow. The bracelet fades when I enter a clearing, so I head back and trudge into another. A lone weeping willow stands in the middle of this clearing, its beautiful tresses sweeping the ground.

I hurry over and slide through the branches, my boots cushioned by a bed of flowers. The sun has already set, but the last of its rays shine over the tree, accentuating the heart-shaped bow carved into the bark.

Murie pauses beside me, struggling to catch her breath. "Is that... is that it?"

"I think so," I say, my heart racing with anticipation. I know I should wait for Hades to do this, but the magic pulling me forward is overwhelming. "I need your help, Murie."

She salutes me jokingly. "Just tell me what to do."

I grin at her. "It's in case I pass out. The first time I touched one of the relics, I lost consciousness. It's like the magic protecting it shocked me or something. Anyway, I just need you to stand close by in case I fall again."

Her expression turns markedly more serious. "Got it."

With the sun bleeding through the willow, I take a deep breath and reach out for the bow. The second I touch the relic, the wood glows like the bracelet on my wrist and a rush of static electricity surges through me. My hair lifts up, turning into snakes that hiss protectively around me, and every ounce of my body pulses with magic. I'm no longer aware of my surroundings as a series of images invade my mind, cutting through my conscience like hot knives.

The ground beneath me trembles and cracks open like an earthquake. The flowers and grass are replaced with blackened soil that has been ravaged by some kind of fire. Wisps of ash float into the air and I lift my gaze to the shadow in the distance. Lava spews out from the mouth of a volcano, but it's alive as arms burst out from the sides and claw their way through the soil. Every movement trembles the earth and yet I remain standing upright as a magical field wraps around my body, protecting me from the chaos.

"Your defiance shall wither and your soul will perish," the creature bellows, spewing a stream of lava that hits me in waves. While the magic protecting me doesn't crack or give way, it weakens as the heat from the lava burns my eyes.

"Who are you? What do you want from me?"

The volcano's mouth cracks open and gurgles fire, almost like it's laughing. "I am Cronos and my destiny is to destroy you and the Dark One..."

As another stream of lava vomits from its mouth, I'm jolted awake, my heart racing in my ears. I look around myself, relieved to find that I'm back in the forest with Murie; the bow lays at my feet, now made of gold.

"Are you alright?" Murie gently touches my arm. "You didn't pass out, but you kind of stood comatose for a moment."

Over the thrashing of my heartbeat, I can hear the panic in her voice. "I'm... I'm okay," I manage shakily. "I just had a vision this time."

My sister stands in front of me. "A vision about what?"

"Of what?"

I look long and hard at her, struggling to put into words what I saw. "I saw a volcano that called itself Cronos."

She tilts her head ever so slightly. "Who the hell is Cronos?"

"I don't know," I say, my hands trembling. "But it said... it said it's going to kill me."

My sister's eyes widen and the blood drains from her face. "I don't think you should keep looking for these relics anymore, Zee. It's becoming dangerous."

I shake my head, determined to find the last one for Mr Knightford. I don't know why; I just feel like I need to. "I'm okay," I tell her firmly. "Besides, it was just a vision. It's not like it's real or anything."

Murie gives me an uncertain look. "Zara—"

"I got the bow!" I bend down to pick it up, then I run my fingers over the gold limbs. "I'd better take this to Mr Knightford."

Before Murie can protest, I turn around and head back to the academy. She follows me wordlessly, but I feel her eyes burning into the back of my head from her concern. I repeat over and over again that the vision wasn't real, that it was just an illusion, but a part of me struggles to believe the words and I can't help but wonder...

Who is Cronos? And why does he want to kill me?

CHAPTER FIFTEEN

The next morning, I wake up to some parchment sliding underneath my door. Phantom jumps off my chest and I hurry over to read the note, brushing my messy hair away from my face.

Snake girl, I've got something cool to
show you. My room. 12C. -Loki

I wonder what he wants to show me? I haven't seen him since the day at the lake. He has since made himself scarce, but I figured he's been busy like me. My heart skips a beat in my chest as I realize how excited I am to see him.

Quietly, to not wake up Murie, I shower and get dressed. I check my reflection in the bathroom mirror. I smooth a hand down my black skin-tight jeans and brush a hair off my chiffon blouse. My pink hair is tucked behind both ears, held in place with a thin black velvet headband, and I tuck a few loose strands away.

Satisfied with my appearance, I leave in search of Loki's room.

The boys' dormitories are much more confusing compared than the girls'. I get lost twice, but thankfully I don't bump into any teachers. I do come across Kal sprawled on a sofa in the common area, his nose buried in a heavy-looking tome.

"Whats up, Zara," he says, saluting me playfully.

I smile at him. "Can you help me find room 12C?"

He raises an eyebrow but doesn't probe me. "Down there, third corridor to your left."

"Thanks." I make my way across the room, then pause. "Congrats on finding the trident. I hope it helps with your mom."

Kal tilts his lips into a crooked smile and inclines his head.

Once I finally locate Loki's room, I take a deep breath and knock three times with my knuckles. I wait and hear his footsteps carrying to the door. Some seconds later, Loki stands in the doorway with a mischievous grin on his face.

He pulls the door wider. "Come forth and enter thy chamber, my lady."

I smirk at him as I step over the threshold, sweeping my gaze around his room. It's larger than mine, and yet there's only one bed. Everything is draped in black and gold silks with emerald soft furnishings, including the fur rug at the foot of his bed and the intricate tapestry hanging on his wall.

"How come you aren't sharing with someone?" I ask, turning to him.

"Perks of being Head Boy."

I walk over to the sofa tucked beneath the huge circular window. "How did you become Head Boy? No offense, but you're hardly the teacher's pet."

"Speaking of pets," he says, ignoring my question completely as he crosses the length of his room. "I thought it was time you met the love of my life."

"Oh," is all I can say as I watch him pull back a curtain. My heart clenches as if a knife has just been cleaved through it. Instead of revealing another window, my gaze lands on a glass terrarium with a beautiful python resting under the heat lamp. The tension that had been building up in my shoulders quickly evaporates and I stand with a grin.

"Is this your snake?" I wiggle my eyebrows at him.

He chuckles, opening the tank to bring her out. "Yes. This is Valkyrie. You can pet her if you want."

Excited, I hurry over and tentatively reach out my hand. Valkyrie is skeptical at first before she slithers toward me and around my hand.

"She's breathtaking," I say, gently stroking her green scales.

"Just like you," Loki counters, no longer smirking or playing with me; he's dead serious now.

I blush at the sincerity of his compliment. "Thanks. She seems to like me. Probably because I'm kind of like her."

"Badass and majestic?" Loki offers, still holding Valkyrie while she susses me out.

"A snake," I giggle, watching as she inspects my bracelet. I'm surprised it hasn't come to life, and neither has my hair. Maybe it's a good thing. I'd rather not freak Valkyrie out and get bitten. Green tree pythons can be a little snappy when provoked, but they're generally quite docile.

Loki watches me closely while I handle her, a great big smile on his face.

"What?" I ask, my cheeks warming under his stare.

"I just like to see you happy like this." Valkyrie works her way back to him and he gently returns her to the enclosure. "You can visit her whenever you like."

I bite my bottom lip and nod. I don't know if I should do this, but he's been so sweet to me...

"Wow!" Loki's eyes widen into emerald orbs that reflect my serpent hair. "Wow," he whispers, reaching out to touch them.

My snakes can sense how at ease I am with him so they don't react negatively. His gaze intent on me, Loki caresses the snake closest to him and she curls around his fingers, her tongue flicking out to gather his scent. As soon as he touches her, I close my eyes and let out a moan, the sound startling me. My eyes shoot open instantly as a rush of heat gathers into my face.

Loki merely smirks. "Does it feel good when I touch them?"

All I can do is nod, words failing me. I've never let anyone touch my cursed hair before, so I had no idea what to expect. One thing I *didn't* expect was for it to feel so damn good.

I close my eyes and cover my face with my hands, a futile effort to hide my embarrassment, but Loki pulls them away and forces me to look at him. He keeps a gentle hold on me while my snakes slither out to inspect him. One of them licks the side of his ear and he just smiles, his eyes warm and gleaming.

"You look even more beautiful like this, Zara."

The air catches in my lungs. "I'm glad you think so."

"I do not think so." He brushes his fingers down my flushed cheek. "I *know* so. I am a god, after all."

"And a villain," I quip, smiling up at him, my heart thrashing like wild pistons in my chest. "I'm not a goddess, though. I'm just all villain."

"You're perfect," he says, and then he's kissing me hard and passionately, his fingers threading through my writhing locks.

I wrap my arms around his neck and reciprocate the kiss with equal ardor. He lifts my legs and hooks me around his waist, carrying me over to the bed. The smell and taste of him are so intoxicating that I forget about my hair as my back presses into the blankets.

Loki towers over me, his hands positioned on either side of my head, and he just looks at me like it's the first time he's really seeing me. I guess in a way, it is the first he's seeing the *real* me; the cursed side my birth parents didn't want.

The cursed side that has Loki's eyes blown with undeniable lust only for me.

He leans down and kisses my collarbone, his hands skimming over my breasts. At a painstakingly slow pace, he unbuttons my blouse while his tongue explores my mouth at a leisurely pace.

I reach for his t-shirt and pull it over his shoulders,

exposing the wide expanse of his torso. His ripped muscles and tapered waistline sculpt him perfectly.

I run my fingers down his chest to the band of his jeans. Now that my blouse has been undone, exposing my breasts, he makes short work of my jeans and yanks them off my body in two swift, effortless moves. At the sight of me not wearing any panties, he looks up and growls, and then he's leaning between my legs, his tongue running gently over my sex. I dig my fingers into the sheets and moan as he spreads my wetness and flicks my clit with dexterous precision. Thank the gods he's a man who knows what to do down there.

And Loki really, *really* does.

I grab the wooden headboard and let go, coming onto his face. His tongue teases and assaults me with pleasure until I'm spent, struggling to catch my breath over the moans he keeps dragging out from me. He laps at me with a fiendish hunger that literally takes my breath away.

My chest rises and falls unevenly as I open my legs further, a silent plea for him to be inside me. He straightens onto his knees and pulls his jeans down, but his movements are stopped when there's a knock on the door.

"Ignore it," I say, running my hand between my legs.

The edge of his lips curve and he wraps a hand around his cock, stroking languidly. However, the knocks become frantic banging, and he groans as he readjusts himself before climbing off the bed. I pull his fur blanket over my body and listen to him opening the door. My heart freezes when I hear Dracula.

"Forgive the intrusion, but I believe my inimă is in there with you."

Loki casts me a glance over his shoulder and then shrugs at Dracula. "You're mistaken. Now piss off."

He attempts to slam the door, but Dracula's leather boot slips over the threshold, blocking him. Before things get ugly, I quickly button my blouse and pull my jeans on.

"I'm here," I say, hurrying over to the door. Loki moves aside but remains in my shadow, watching closely. "What's wrong, Drac?"

"Kal said you were here. I had hoped he was wrong..." Dracula's gaze slides over my shoulders to Loki, narrowing into slits. He looks back at me and his glare softens. "Will you come with me a moment?"

I glance back at Loki, who frowns. "Actually, we were about to—"

"Please, inimă?"

His plea catches me off guard, and I find myself nodding before I even know what I'm doing.

"Okay," I say, mouthing sorry to Loki before I disappear entirely.

However, he's no longer looking at me.

CHAPTER SIXTEEN

"**I** had no idea there was a cemetery here," I say, rubbing the chill from my arm with one hand as rain falls lightly onto my red umbrella.

Dracula shoves his shoulder into the wrought-iron gate. "It's where anyone who dies on the island gets buried."

With a final shove, the gate opens and he motions for me to step through. My boots sink into the damp, nearly trimmed grass, and I slide my gaze around the cemetery.

Dracula scans the headstones bathed in slivers of sunlight clawing through the black clouds. "What a dreary evening," he says, a smile tilting his pale lips.

"I know. Isn't it wonderful?" I return the smile and step further inside. "I'm glad I came out with you."

He falls into step with me. "You are?"

I nod, pointing to the small bench outside a mausoleum shrouded in ivy. "Shall we sit here?"

Dracula hurries over and wipes the bench with the

sleeve of his ash-grey blazer. I smile at him and settle down on the bench, shimmying closer when he sits beside me so that we're both sheltered by the umbrella. For a long while we're silent and just watch the rain splash the puddles covering the ground.

I peek at him from under my lashes, and the muscles clenching hard on his jaw concern me. There's something deeply troubling him and now I'm glad I agreed to come here. He clearly needs to get something off his chest.

"Drac, are you okay?"

He turns his head to look at me, his eyes no longer red but a deep, swirling black. "No," he whispers, then looking back at the gravestones. "I'm troubled by an issue that has begun bleeding into the lives of those I care about."

I keep my voice low, but it still shakes a little. "Whose lives? What issue? Talk to me, Drac..."

His gaze still averted from me, he answers, "It's about my father."

"I thought Daddy Drac had something to do about it."

Dracula's eyes snap to me. "*Don't.*"

I swallow hard, regretting using the nickname; it was just meant to be a joke. His expression softens a little when he catches my glimmer of unease.

"My father... is a difficult vampire. I have no rela-tionship with him, but I am still his only heir and it's my duty to take over his empire in Transylvania." He glances at me and then forward again. A rose flutters in the breeze, its petals brushing the headstone in front of us. "I have no interest in doing this. If I had my way, I would leave for the other side of the world and never see him again."

"Is this why you came to the academy?" I ask softly, "to get away from him?"

"Yes, and no. The academy is the only place I'm spared of my father and his... unethical ways. But I can't stay here forever. Vampires age slowly compared to mortals, so my time here is just a week in the eyes of my father. Soon I'll have to go home and continue preparation for when he steps down and passes everything over to me."

He pauses, as if searching for the right words to say next. "I also came here to, in some way, atone for what I did that night."

"Alena," I say quietly.

"Yes. I met her when I was last sent here. After months of dating, she... she walked out to the lake and drowned herself." His eyes flick down to the ring on his finger, the same one his dad wears. "But it was not of her own accord. It was my *father's*!" He spits the last word out, his tone rising several octaves while a dark shadow drifts over his features. "I should've known. I was a fool. I'd seen the signs, the way he looked at her on visitation days... the same way he looked at you."

I know exactly what he's talking about. His dad looked at me like I was filth clinging to his expensive leather shoes. And he caused Alena's death? My stomach recoils at the thought.

"What do you mean it was your dad's fault that Alena drowned? Did he do it?"

Dracula's jaw clenches hard for a second, his eyes focus on the rose. "Yes. He compelled her to walk into the lake. I... I tried stopping her." He looks at me, his anger contorting into sheer panic. "I chased her through the forest to the lake, but by the time I dragged her out, she was gone. You must believe me when I say it wasn't my fault."

I reach out for his hand, my gesture apparently startling him. "I believe you."

He releases a breath. "I did everything I could, but it was too late. Everyone saw me holding her dead body. The headmaster believed me when I said she was under a spell, but nobody else did. I deserved their hatred. If I hadn't shown interest in her, my father would've left her alone."

"Why is he like this? It's barbaric."

"It is. And he's this way toward anyone who is not a vampire. To him, vampires and mortals should never mix. They're just disposable bags of blood in his eyes."

"That's disgusting," I say, shuddering at his father's grotesqueness.

Dracula nods, looking at me. "I thought I loved Alena even when every vampire around me forbade it. But as soon as I saw you, Zara, I realised I wasn't *in* love with her. Not like I am with you."

My heart rate accelerates. "You love me?" I echo, my voice just above a whisper.

"With every bit of my cold, un-beating heart." He says the words so confidently and calmly that my heart clenches. "I haven't been able to get you out of my mind from the moment I saw you in the cafeteria that day.

And yet I..." Now he looks away, his eyebrows drawing together. "I can't be with you."

My heart doesn't just increase in tempo this time—it sky-rockets before plummeting to the pit of my stomach. A lump rises in my throat, cutting off my ability to speak, and I wrestle the tears threatening to gather in my eyes.

"It's my father," he says quietly. "The thought of him hurting you... because of how I feel for you..." He shakes his head vigorously. "It's incomprehensible. I can't do it. I *won't.*"

Balancing the umbrella against the back of the bench, I lift his hands and clasp them gently within mine. Dracula turns to me, his eyes veiled with a darkness I've never seen in them before.

"I just don't want to hurt you, Zara."

I swallow the nerves threatening to tremble my lower lip. The pain in his voice is just too much. "Hey, I'm a big girl. I can look after myself," I say softly, giving him a smile intended to be reassuring, but his face remains somber. "Is there anything we can do to convince your dad otherwise?"

I feel stupid asking it, considering his dad killed the last girl he dated. But when a flicker of hesitation skims over Dracula's features, my hope grows ever so slightly.

"There is something, isn't there?" I squeeze his hands. "Tell me."

He takes a sharp inhale through his nose. "The only way we can be together," he says, the timbre of his voice dropping to a gruff whisper, "is if you become my bride. Then my father will be unable to harm you because once you and I are bonded, we become one, and my father will risk no harm to me. He's too selfish to jeopardize his empire that way."

I blink and stare hard at him, my eyes so large they almost pop out from my skull. "Wait a minute. Did you just say *bride*?"

He nods grimly. "You're my inimă. Your heart is my heart; I knew it the moment I saw you. My father knew it, too, which is why he hasn't interfered. Instead, he gave me an ultimatum. Either I take you as my bride or I let you go."

"But if you let me go..." I trail off, searching for the right words. "Letting me go means you'll never have your inimă, right? That your heart will never beat?"

Again he nods, although this time hesitantly. "Precisely. However, your life means more to me than anything, and if letting you go is what it takes to protect you, I'll do it even if it kills me."

I look down at our joined hands, struggling to comprehend and respond to all this. My gaze darts around the cemetery as if seeking answers to questions I am unable to ask; questions I'm scared of even thinking about.

I've never let myself love anyone before. Sure, I feel things for Dracula, Loki, and even Hades, but love? I thought it was just lust. And yet a part of me blooms beneath all the wilted flowers and weeds that had weighed me down my entire life. I claw my way through them, dragging the weeds off to reveal that section of my heart that always remained out of touch, hidden behind a sheet of glass. And I smash right through it.

"I never thought I'd become your bride after only one date, but..." I bite my lower lip, nodding at him with an utter conviction I feel deep within my soul. "I want to be with you, Drac."

The dark veil shrouding his features slips away, at the same moment the sun appears from behind the clouds, bathing us in its light. "You truly mean that? Do you truly want that? Being my bride means we are bonded until death parts us."

"Then even when I'm dead, we'll still be together because vampires live forever. Right?"

Dracula chuckles and brushes his thumb over the top of my hand. "Right."

I ignore the thrashing of my heart and nod at him. "Okay, then tell me what to do. Should I put on a veil and walk down the aisle or...?"

Dracula shakes his head, a grin tugging his lips. "Not quite. If you agree to become my bride, I will bind us by drinking your blood. This is not the official ceremony, but it is enough to prevent my father from intervening." He holds my hands, his eyes darkening. "I want you to know that if you agree to do this, that if you want it and I taste your blood, as soon as we're free from this academy, I'm marrying you, Zara, and claiming you as my bride the vampire way. It's not something that can ever be reversed. There is still time for you to reconsider. You don't have to—"

I press my finger against his lips to silence him. "I

want this. You want this. So what the fuck are you waiting for? Bite me already."

His lips spread into a grin against my finger. With a nod, he pushes off the bench and kneels at my feet. The rain falls lightly onto his shoulders and the puddle beneath him soaks through his trousers. He holds out a hand, almost like he's proposing, which would make sense given the whole vampire bride thing. Slowly I place my hand in his and he runs his fingers along my wrist, the touch tickling me.

"Beautiful," he whispers, studying the blood coursing through my veins. "How insanely beautiful."

I'm pinned under his stare, unable to breathe let alone look away from him. I'm so caught up in the moment that I don't ask him if it will hurt when he bites me. All I can focus on is him—us—and the thought of being together forever. It's enough to drown out the reality of pain.

Dracula doesn't even look away from me when he leans forward and runs his fangs down my arm to the veins fluttering in my wrist. He kisses me there, his lips cold and gentle, and my heart soars into a dance in my chest.

Gods, what am I doing? Why do I want this? I'm about to become Dracula's bride...

When his fangs pierce my skin, I hold my breath to stifle the cry that tries to escape me. My heart lurches as the veins in my arm burn as though filled with fire. It's painful, but not enough that I want him to stop. His gaze intent on my own holds me in a tight caress, binding me so that I cannot move. I puncture my lip with my teeth to keep from making any noise. The way he looks up at me, as if I'm everything to him, is the most intoxicating thing in the world.

Carefully his fangs sink lower into my flesh, and my blood pours into his mouth. All the while he drinks from me, his efforts growing frantic and hungrier, his eyes remain rooted on mine. It's the lust in his gaze that soothes my discomfort. The pain almost transcends into something pleasurable, beautiful even, the more he kisses and suckles me. His gaze darkens with every droplet of blood that filters onto his tongue. He closes his eyes and his moan vibrates against my wrist, tingling all the way up my arm.

I can feel him tethering himself to me. It's like he's casting a lasso around my heart and binding me to him. My heart beats twice as fast now, and yet it feels no different to me.

I really am Dracula's heart. His inimă.

"*Mirific, inimă mea,*" he whispers in Romanian, slowly pulling his lips away. Two small incisions remain in their place, but as soon as Dracula kisses them, the blood stops flowing. However, not before his lips stain a vibrant red and dark veins shoot out around his eye sockets. "*De necrezut...* Just wonderful."

Holding my breath, I watch him stand before he lifts me to my feet. My umbrella topples to the ground and the rain splashes us gently as he pulls me to him. Ever so softly, his lips claim mine, and the sharp coppery tang of my blood, mingled with the scent and taste of Dracula, is strangely alluring.

He traces his fingers down the side of my face,

murmuring over and over again "my inimă", while his other hand presses over my heart. The double-beat is foreign and yet so intrinsic that I barely register it, like it's always beat for two souls instead of one.

"Drac, that was..." I trail off, struggling to find the right words. "Just wonderful."

He grins, his fingers brushing my lips.

The tender moment is interrupted when Hades, followed by a sulking Loki, steps out from the bushes. They glare at Dracula wiping the droplets of blood from the corners of his mouth. It's Loki who deduces what happened first.

"You bloodsucking motherfucker—" He jumps forward, his fists raised, but Hades stands in the way.

"Enough," he growls. "We didn't come here to fight."

My heart lurching against my ribs, I ask, "Why *did* you come here?"

Loki's nostrils flare as he takes a step back and slowly unclenches his fists. "Your lover boy Hades told me you needed my help to find one of the relics."

Lover boy? I raise my eyebrow at that before looking at Hades. "This is supposed to be our quest. Why is Loki getting involved?"

"Because I found a riddle about the sword in the headmaster's book," Hades answers, his tone remains unaltered despite the unpleasant look on his face. He holds the book up and nods to Loki. "The Asgardian was able to help decipher it since it had some Norse influence. We finally know where the sword is."

Dracula tugs my hand, concern etched deeply on his face. "What sword? What relics is he talking about?"

Loki scoffs loudly and crosses his arms. "Oh, didn't she tell you? Now that *is* interesting."

"That's enough, Loki," I warn him, frustrated by the way he's antagonizing Dracula after what he promised me.

"What relics?" Dracula repeats softly, his frown deepening.

Once I'm finished telling him about the Four Horsemens' relics, he reaches for my umbrella and lifts it over my head. "I'm coming with you. Where you go, I go, inimă."

Even though Loki continues scoffing and Hades just rolls his eyes, I smile at Dracula and link my fingers with his. Searching for the final relic with all three of my guys is definitely not going to be easy, but I'm truly happy that they're coming with me this time. Hopefully, they don't kill each other in the process.

CHAPTER SEVENTEEN

do my best to keep the peace between my guys. However, the tension is so intense that I could penetrate it with a knife.

"So, umm, where are we going?" I ask, hoping to break the silence, my fingers still twined with Dracula's.

"I'm so glad you asked." Loki winks over his shoulder at me and takes the book from Hades. "We are going to the Hollow Cave at this tip of the island."

"A cave?" Dracula echoes. "I didn't know there were caves here."

"Shows what you know," Loki all but grumbles. "That's why I'm here to help save the day." He looks right at me when he says this, and I can't help but roll my eyes at him. Really now.

"Well, we're doing this as a team," I say, looking at Loki and Hades in particular. "How much farther until we reach the cave?"

Loki points north through the trees. "Not much. There's a mountain about a mile or so that way."

One of many awkward silences later, we approach the mountainside. Loki leads the way until he finds the entrance carved into the jagged rock.

"Just as I remember," he says, running his hands over the stone. When he turns to me, he couldn't look more smug even if he tried. "See. I'm not just a pretty face, you know."

Hades marches past him and enters the cave, but I remain stagnant by the entrance.

"Umm. I don't know about you, Drac, but I don't really fancy entering a creepy dark cave without knowing what's in there."

He nods in agreement, training his pinched gaze on Loki. "What awaits us? I will not have my inimă put in harm's way."

Loki's eyes narrow into shards. "You really think I'd risk hurting her? She's not yours, bloodsucker, and she never fucking will be, no matter how much of her blood you drink."

Yikes. I was wrong when I thought the tension couldn't possibly get any worse.

"Okay, okay." I hold my hands up in a placating gesture. "Let's stay focused for now. I really need to get this relic so we can help protect the academy." Turning to Loki, I ask, "What's in the cave?"

Hades appears at my side, cutting in before Loki can answer. "The sword is visible only in sunlight, so it can't be too far inside."

I look around the entrance for anything shiny. The

cave is dark and dusty, a place where a sword should stand out, but I can't see anything and my bracelet isn't reacting.

"What else did the riddle say?" Dracula demands, his grip tightening on my hand just a fraction.

Loki mutters something foreign under his breath, then he speaks in English. "It said the sword needs the strength of three to free it. Not. Four. So why don't you just stand there like a good fucking vampire and shut up?"

"Enough!" I snap, unable to tolerate this anymore. "Remember what we talked about in your room?"

He shrugs. "I said I wouldn't kill him. I didn't say I'd treat him with respect. He's as good as a dog to me."

Dracula laughs, releasing my hand to step forward. "Then you better watch that tongue of yours, Loki of Asgard, or I'll gladly bite it off."

"Ladies!" Hades growls, his hair glowing vibrant blue with rage. I've never seen it do that before. Then again, I've never really seen him mad before. "We're here to find a fucking sword. Quit with the fighting and help Zara complete this quest."

To my surprise, this has an effect on them because they both look away. I breathe a sigh and mouth thank you to Hades as I walk by him, scanning the cave for the sword. It takes about ten minutes of searching the entrance before we finally locate the relic. The gold hilt pokes out from an enormous rock buried into the ground.

"That's some Sword in the Stone bullshit right

there," Loki says and the three of us nod in agreement. "Allow me, gentlemen."

With an amused grin, I watch Loki rotate his neck, crack his knuckles and stroll confidently forward before attempting to pry the sword from the stone. Of course, it doesn't work.

"You said it requires the strength of three," Dracula points out, crossing his arms. "You possess only the strength of one if you are lucky."

Loki shrugs, not even bothering to glare at him this time. "I was loosening it for your weak ass self."

With a shake of my head, I march after him. Dracula and Hades follow in my wake, each taking a corner of the stone, and I look down at the gilded hilt shining in the sunlight.

"On three," Hades says, reaching for the sword. "One... two..."

"Oh, I should probably mention that I may pass out," I warn Dracula and Loki. "It doesn't always happen. Last time I just got a vision."

"And the time before that she almost drowned," Hades bites out, his lips thinning into a grim line. "So be careful and keep an eye on her."

Both Dracula and Loki look hard at me.

"Perhaps we shouldn't do this." Dracula stands back, silently imploring me to do the same.

I don't.

"Yeah. Who needs a bunch of old relics, anyway?" Loki waves a hand at the ancient sword like it's nothing. "I've got plenty of them back home."

Touched by their concern over me, I smile and

shake my head. "No. I promised Mr Knightford I'd do this."

"Why did you promise?" Dracula's question echoes around us, clearly directed at me.

I stare down at the sword, searching for the right answer. I've never really thought about why I'm doing this. Is it because I want to help the headmaster protect the academy despite the fact that I don't even want to be here? Or is it because I hope finding them will bring me closer to the man who created me?

Mr Knightford is my biological dad, and yet I barely know anything about him. I've been so focused on finding these relics that I've not spent any time with him. In a way, I thought finding them would give us an opportunity to bond and get to know each other.

"I want to help protect the academy," I decide to reply, too conflicted by which answer to choose since my reason for doing this is a mix of the two of them. I guess I don't want them to know Mr Knightford is my real dad yet.

If the guys disagree with me, they don't voice it, but they do nod and step forward again. Hades nods and once more counts down from three. The second he says the last digit, we each grab hold of the sword and pull.

My bracelet slithers around the hilt and connects to it as if it was created for this sword. The moment it locks into place, a blinding white light blasts my eyes, and images flood through my mind in rapid, crystal-clear succession.

I'm draped in a silver gown that trails the earth at my

bare feet. A crown of flowers adorns my long, flowing pink hair. I'm much older as I walk through the bustling meadow, each footstep leaving a trail of petals in my wake. Standing beneath an archway wrapped in black ivy is Hades, except he's older, too, and his silk robes are unlike anything I've ever seen. They move around him like tendrils of smoke and his hair is also long, the blue tresses resting just above his waist. A black crown sits on top of his head and his eyes shimmer like molten gold as he watches me walk down the aisle to him.

The next vision is just the two of us. Hades takes me into his arms and kisses me deeply, passionately, in a beautiful chamber carved from black quartz that glitter in the pale moonlight.

"My ilios," he whispers, looking into my eyes with infinite adoration.

I look up at him with the same amount of unconditional love. "My astéri."

More visions flood through me, each more powerful than the last. Laughing with Hades, walking through the forest with him, holding his hand, kissing his lips, whispering words of eternal love for each other—it was all real.

This was my life with Hades.

A final scene enters my mind, and fear instantly clogs my throat. Cronos, the Titan who despised me for rejecting him for Hades, breaks through the gates to my home in the Underworld. Hades takes my hand and rushes onto the balcony of our chamber. Despite the tears racing down my cheeks, I look up at him with complete and utter acceptance of our fate. His hand rests on my stomach and he kisses me before we leap off the balcony together, wrapped in each other's arms.

The scream tearing from my lips drags me back into reality. I let go of the sword and stumble back. Strong hands catch me before I fall, and I look up at Hades. His expression softens as if he realizes that I can finally see again.

That I can finally see *him.*

I reach up to cup his face and tears spring to his eyes when I touch him. He places his hand over mine and then kisses me. No words are shared between us in this moment of revelation. No words are needed. After everything we've gone through in this life and the last, we're together again. Nothing will ever be able to part us. Not Cronos. Not Gaia. No one, no thing.

"We got it," Loki snarls, dumping the sword down beside us. "Sorry to interrupt the tender moment."

I look away from Hades and up at Loki and Dracula. They're both watching me with equal amounts of unease. When I look at them, I still feel the love I possessed before I regained my memories. Nothing will ever change how I feel about them. It's just changed how I feel about Hades.

"I'm sorry for pushing you into the lake," I say to him, my voice quiet.

He just chuckles and caresses my hand. "I would have endured it a thousand times over until you remembered me."

The tears I've been holding back slip from my eyes. I straighten up to kiss him, my love, my husband, my astéri, my soul mate, and for a moment the entire world slips away. It's just the two of us, reunited at last. I'm only pulled out of the sweet reverie when Dracula clears his throat.

Hades gently lifts me off the floor. My feet barely touch the ground when he hisses and clutches his arm and stomach.

"Hades?" I tenderly reach for his arm, but he avoids me by bending over to retrieve the sword.

"Let's go, my love," he says, taking my hand in his free one.

I know when Hades is hiding something from me, and he's doing exactly that right now. As I follow him out of the cave, I make a mental note to discuss this with him once we're alone. We have so much to discuss. So much hurt and pain and years lost between us.

And Cronos.

The vision I had of the Titan makes sense now. He's still lurking in the shadows, waiting to strike one last time.

I clutch tighter onto Hades as reality sinks in. Cronos knows where we are. We need to defeat him before he defeats us. However, we need to first return the sword to my mortal father, Mr Knightford. Once we've done that, we can figure out what to do.

For the entire journey back to the academy, Loki and Dracula remain several meters apart, each of them uncharacteristically quiet. Nobody says a word even when we reach Mr Knighford's office and Hades presents the sword to him.

"We obtained all four of the relics," he says, his grip

weakening on my hand. He's grown considerably paler since we reached the academy and it's beginning to worry me. As soon as we leave here, I'll take him to the infirmary.

"What do we do now?" I ask Mr Knightford, glancing at the other relics laid out on the desk before him.

The headmaster stands from his chair and takes the sword from Hades.

However, the second Hades lets go, his hand slips from mine and he collapses onto the floor.

CHAPTER EIGHTEEN

Mr Knightford places the sword on his desk and kneels on the floor beside me. I gently place Hades' head into my lap, but he falls limp in my arms as the veins pulsing in his neck blacken and spread over him. My hands trembling, I yank open his shirt and gasp at the sight of all the dark veins writhing over his torso. All this time, he hasn't been enduring 'a little pain': he's been poisoned.

"Hades!" I shout his name, but my voice barely comes out a whisper. "Hades, my love, please don't leave me… Please don't go!"

"Be careful, Zara," Mr Knightford warns.

Loki bends down beside the headmaster. "What's happening to him?"

Meanwhile, Dracula runs out into the hallway and shouts for help. It's like I'm aware of all these things happening around me and yet all I can seem to focus on is him, only Hades. Somewhere deep inside, I know he's dying in my arms and I'm powerless to save him.

"There is nothing we can do for him," Mr Knightford says, and I shake my head, refusing to accept this answer. After everything Hades and I have endured, I cannot lose him.

Not again.

No!

Hades slowly blinks his eyes open. When he smiles up at me, just faintly, tears leak furiously from my eyes and splash his cheeks. "Don't cry," he whispers.

"What's — what's happening to you?"

"The underworld..." He coughs and winces at the pain. "The underworld is returning me."

"I don't understand, my love."

"The relics," Loki says, piecing it all together. "They must have triggered something that's dragging him back to the Underworld."

"Yes." Mr. Knightford nods grimly. "I believe that is the case."

"No..." Again I shake my head, unable to stop from doing so. "It can't be. This *can't* be happening!"

Dracula falls down beside me and places a hand on my shoulder. "Perhaps there is time to save him."

"H-how?" The word barely leaves my lips as tears race violently down my cheeks.

"I can turn him," he says, his fangs extending like an unsheathed blade. "He will become a vampire like me, but he'll still be alive. There isn't much time, we must—"

Hades shakes his head, cutting Dracula off. "It won't work... I had only a limited time... in this world.

Nothing that can be done… the Underworld is calling me home."

The poison spreads even more quickly, first to his legs, then his chest and neck, leaving only part of his face untouched. I grip him harder, refusing to let him go, to accept this. We died for each other. He will *not* die alone.

"Hades, you can't go. We made a promise. You and me, for eternity." My tears race down my cheeks in a violent torrent that soaks through his shirt. "I can't live in this world or any other without you. Please, don't go…"

He opens his eyes, but they're almost black now. "It's my time, ílios." His hand falls limply upon mine. "I'm just glad… you remembered me… one last time."

A pain I've never known before slices its way through me. I open my mouth to tell Hades that I love him and I will never let him. However, the moment that I do, the poison covers his eyes, and he's gone.

My grief pours out from the depths of my being. I scream as I hold him in my arms, wishing and praying to all the gods and goddesses in existence to bring my love back to me. My tears splash onto his face, mixing with the darkness that took him away from me. How can this be our ending? How? *How*?!

"Zara, look at him."

Dracula's voice barely registers in my mind, I'm so consumed by the pain tearing me asunder. My heart feels like it's been smashed into a million little pieces and then crushed into dust for good measure. Still, I manage to open my eyes, and the air leaves my lungs when I see what's happening to Hades. Each teardrop that escapes my lashes and lands on him slowly erases the darkness within his veins. At first it's just a droplet or two, but then my tear stains begin to glow a blinding gold that sinks into his body.

"Hades?" I press my lips to his, hoping it will wake him, and my world trembles when I feel him kissing me back. "You're *alive!*"

"Such a pity," Mr Knightford drawls, pulling my attention away from Hades.

"What?" I look around for the headmaster. Although I can't see him, I can hear his voice whispering a strange incantation that is foreign to my ears and yet not quite. Words here and there make sense to me… words of darkness and revenge and unparalleled power.

Dracula and Loki stand in front of me, almost like they're forming a protective shield, but I gaze through their legs and watch Mr Knightford consume each of the Four Horsemens' relics in thick tendrils of magic.

Dark, forbidden magic.

"What are you doing?" Loki demands, his scepter appearing in his hand.

I wrap my arms tighter around Hades and back up to the wall as far as I can. We can only watch in horror as wave after wave of black magic pours out from relics and into Mr Knightford's body. His clothes shred off him like wet paper and his features contort hideously, transforming into something entirely different.

Something sinister and monstrous.

"He's morphing," Hades says, his voice weak. "We need to get out of here."

It's already too late. Mr Knightford has shapeshifted into a different creature entirely—one I have never seen in this life before and yet it is one I know all too well.

"Cronos." His name trembles on my lips as violently as the rest of my body. "All this time, you were Cronos?"

His lips twist into a sinister snarl. "Yes, and now you will suffer my wrath once and for all. There is no escape from me this time, Persephone… only pain and permanent death."

To Be Continued…

ABOUT THE AUTHOR

Scarlett Snow comes from a big family in a small Scottish town and has always strived to prove that if you are passionate about something, no one can stop you from chasing your dreams. She lives with her wolf dog and kitties and is unashamedly addicted to coffee.

If you'd like to join her NEWSLETTER to be kept updated on her books, you can do so here: www.scarlett.katzesnow.com

FOLLOW SCARLETT

Facebook Reader's Group: https://www.facebook.com/groups/scarlettscoven

Facebook Page: https://www.facebook.com/authorscarlettsnow

Amazon: https://www.amazon.com/Scarlett-Snow/e/B07NKFPSKN

Excerpt from Shadowborn Academy (Dark Fae
Academy Series: Book One)

Buy Here

ABOUT THIS BOOK
(Complete series)

**My fate is in the dark,
And my shadow there is real...**

The darkness likes to play in this world.
It also likes to deceive.

In the Enchanted Forest, secrets thrive and one girl
desperately needs to find answers before it's too late.
That girl is Corvina Charles, a powerful Shadowborn—
a human who touched dark magic and became
something else.

Something dangerous.

At the age of eighteen, Corvina and her best friend are swept away to the Shadowborn Academy, the one place where magic and darkness coincide.

It's also where pupils go missing, teachers don't play by any rules, the therapist is hot, and boys with dark magic love to seduce your soul.

With death becoming a game at the academy that not even the Dark or Light Fae seem capable of winning, Corvina's love life should really be the last thing on her mind…especially when one of the boys just so happens to be her teacher!

Shadowborn Academy is a Dark Reverse Harem Paranormal Fae Romance for 18+. In this world, not even the shadows can be trusted…

Chapter One
Corvina

The moonlight bleeding through the trees creates flickering shadows that dance around me. I should be afraid of them like all the other children are, but I'm not. These shadows are safe. They're not like the ones watching me from the treetops, waiting to snatch me off the ground.
No, these shadows are different.
They're my friends.
The faeries hiding in them follow me like they always do

when I come into the Enchanted Forest. I can't see them but I can hear them giggling and whispering in my ear. They flick my dark curly hair over my shoulders and play with the ribbons on my light blue dress, then the frills of my white socks with the little bunny rabbits on them. It's their way of saying hello and it makes me giggle as I skip through the forest, humming to the song Mama always sings to me before I go to sleep.

Mama and Papa warned me not to follow these faeries. They said they're not like the rest and I'll be in deep trouble if I ever go out to play after dark. That's when the faeries come out. They sing to children like me and promise us things beyond our wildest dreams, but nobody ever sees them again once they follow the faeries into the forest. Mama said it's because they gobble them up for supper. I don't believe her. I mean, how horrible would that be? I don't think we taste very nice.

Pitch said the real reason the children don't come back is magical.

He told me that they grow wings and go to live with the faeries. He said I can do that, too, once I make my wish. I'm so excited. I can hear him singing to me and I start humming along to his favourite song, the one about the raven and the wishing well. I follow his voice, excited to play with him again and eat snacks and tell each other stories. No one else can see or hear Pitch apart from me and the faeries. Although we're the same age, he doesn't look like any of the boys from my village. He's extremely pale with glowing amber eyes and long ebony hair that sways around him like the shadows do in here. I know he's different and that's why I like him.

That's why I'm following him.

Now that it's my eighth birthday, Pitch is going to let me make a wish in the well he sings about. He says only special humans—the chosen ones—get to make a wish here. Sometimes he says funny things like that and I don't understand him. All I want is a pair of shiny blue shoes, the same ones as my dolly. Pitch says the faeries are going to give them to me, and then I'll finally have the same outfit as my little dolly.

The faeries guide me to the edge of a clearing which is bright from the moonlight shining down. I wave goodbye to them, even though I can't see where they are, then I continue humming and skipping after Pitch.

I can see him now, sitting on top of the well, and my heart soars as I race through the clearing. Once I reach the well, he lifts me onto the stone with him. It's wide enough that the two of us can stand together without falling into the hole.

"It's time to make your wish," he says, and my stomach fills with butterflies. "Are you ready to be born again?" I don't know what he means by that; I just want the lovely shoes. I nod anyway, and Pitch smiles at me. "Then close your eyes."

When I do this, I hold my breath, too excited to breathe.

My heart feels like it's going to burst out from my chest. I feel dizzy and sick and excited.

"Do you remember what we talked about?" Pitch asks quietly. "What you do once you make your wish? It's very important that you don't forget that part."

"I won't forget," I tell him firmly, peeking through my eyelashes. "Can I say it now? Can I make my wish?"

He giggles and lets go of my hand. "Go on, Corvina. Make your wish and make it count."

I let out an excited squeal, then I scrunch up my little face and think really hard because I don't want to mess this up.

—Hello faeries! Please can I have the same shoes as my dolly? You know, the sparkly blue shoes with the pretty bows on the silver buckles? I would like them very much. Thank you.—

With my wish uttered, I open my eyes. Pitch is gone just like he said he would be and I'm alone on the well. I look down into the tunnel of darkness stretching before me. A loose pebble falls away from the edge and drops into the well. It takes forever to splash through the water at the bottom, and I gulp, my palms turning sweaty against my dress.

For my wish to come true, I need to go down there.

Pitch said he'll be waiting for me and that the faeries will even give me wings so that I don't hurt myself. I'll be just like the other children who followed the faeries into the woods and lived happily ever after. Maybe I'll even be able to see my friends, Bella and Michael and Agnes.

We'll all be faeries together, like we used to talk about.

I turn around and spread my arms out like wings, smiling at the thought of seeing my friends from school again. Taking a deep breath and holding it in my chest, I close my eyes and fall down into the well, praying that Mama and Papa were wrong about the faeries, and about Pitch, the monster hiding under my bed...

Before I plunge to my death, I wake up with a gasp for air, crutching my thin bedsheets in my hands. Pitch wasn't waiting for me. There was nothing but pain and misery at the bottom of that stupid well and my innocent ass didn't know any better back then.

I fell into magical darkness, and as everyone here tells me, that's when I became a shadowborn.

But that's not the part that haunts me every night in my dreams. Oh, no. It's what happened after the pain and misery—after I drowned in all the magical water, my eight-year-old body absorbing it like it was sugar and I was a starving kid. When my heart started beating again and I opened my eyes, I lay floating on my back as the moon drew closer and closer to me. I remember crying and thinking I had been turned into a bug instead of a faery, but it was just the water healing my shattered bones and floating me up to the surface.

The second my feet touched the earth again, my power exploded and I destroyed everything in a five-mile radius, including all the houses and the people inside them.

Including my parents.

And the only living thing was me, covered in ash, lying on the forest floor as the sun rose into a blood-red sky.

Talk about a birthday to remember.

After that, I was picked up by the Shadow Wardens, protectors of the magical world, and thrown in a shadowborn foster home with all the other children that are like me. Only they didn't kill hundreds of people and not one of them in here see their powers like the curses really are.

"You having those dreams again?" Sage asks, sitting

up on her bed next to me and staring at me, the moon-light highlighting her beige skin and curly pink hair that isn't at all messy even though she just woke up. Sage Millhouse is the only bit of this foster home that I've ever cared about and I'm certain it's the same way for her. We came here on the same day, two scared kids who wanted nothing more than to escape this hellhole and the new powers we have. Sage got her power the way most of the kids here did, by being bitten by a shadowborn in their animal state. One bite is enough to infuse any soul with shadow magic, and all it took for Sage was a bite from a fox in her garden.

The fox was never seen again, and Sage nearly died, only to survive and be taken from her parents to come and live here.

The foster home is full of those stories, and it's the main reason I don't talk about my past.

"Always."

It's all I need to say for Sage to get off her bed and head out of the room. I follow her, the old wooden floorboards creaking under my bare feet with each step. Sage holds the timber door open and we head outside into the garden. The cool air is refreshing for only a second before it's nothing but cold nipping at my skin.

"Ready?" I ask her as I stare up, the darkness and shadows comforting me like they always do.

Sage doesn't reply, though I'm unsurprised as she isn't one for words. That's why I like her. I watch her bright purple eyes as she disappears in a cloud of black smoke. The darkness. It's become a blanket of sorts to people like us. As the blackness fades away, there is nothing more than a hawk sitting on the ground, its lavender eyes staring up at me. I grin as I close my own silver eyes and do the next best thing in the world.

I let the darkness take me, creating me into something more.

Something so much better than I already am.

My body disappears into the darkness but my mind always stays, loving the comfort as I shift into a raven and follow Sage into the skies of Blackpool.

Chapter Two
Corvina

"We should head back," Sage suggests around a spoonful of ice cream.

I watch the sea lap at the steps beside the shore and the sandbags lined at the top of them. The skies are grey, eerily so, like they can sense what a crap day this is going to be for us. The sea smells of salt and I can almost taste it over the bubblegum lollipop I've just finished off. Over the sounds of the waves, the seagulls make themselves known with loud squeaks, and in the distance, some children ride bikes down the front.

"Why? I have nothing to pack and neither do you. The wardens aren't coming until nightfall," I remind her. She eyes me carefully and I try to pick up on her emotions. Is she as nervous as me? Unlikely. The Shadowborn Academy is our next home, starting from tonight. We both have known we would attend this year, on the year we turn eighteen, since we aren't classed as kids anymore. The academy is meant to teach us control and endurance, to accept our new life and fit into their society of normal magics.

What if you don't want to fit in?

I asked our warden that once, and she laughed like it was the funniest thing in the world.

"They might not come for us at all. Wouldn't that be nice?" she replies, and I smirk at her, leaning back on the bench. I chuck the stick of my ice lolly in the bin and go back to people watching the streets.

I love people watching, and so does Sage. We have spent days on this bench, making up stories for random strangers we spot. Our stories are unlikely to be right, but it gives us an escape into a normal world —a world where our nightmares cannot reach us. We can almost pretend we're just two teenagers skipping school instead of what we really are.

"Do you think Keeper Maddox will miss us?" Sage asks, her voice dripping with humour.

The Light Warden runs our foster home and she's the fourth one since I came here, as all the others quit. No one likes looking after dozens of kids with shadow powers, and all of whom want their parents back. These poor wardens would literally prefer any other assignment in the magics world. It's depressing, but Keeper Maddox isn't the worst of the lot.

"I doubt she will even notice us leave. She prefers the younger ones," I reply.

They're easier to control.

As for me and Sage?

We're damaged goods and a waste of air. Or so

we've been told by previous wardens. Sometimes late at night, when my demons catch up with me, I almost believe them.

~

"And you have your book? In the name of Selena, do not forget that book, child," Keeper Maddox warns me later that day, giving my opened trunk an assessing once over. Spotting the old, tattered book beside my trunk, she nods. "Thank the Gods. You mustn't forget it. Always have your book with you—"

"—from the instant you enter the forest," I tersely interject, having endured this spiel many times before now. "The book is our bible. We get it, Miss Maddox."

We've had no choice but to.

I've read the *Book of Zorya* a million times already. I don't know why she'd think we'd leave here without it. It's practically the map to our new home. A home neither of us wants to be part of.

Well, Sage says she doesn't, but I have a sneaky suspicion she's excited to use magic beyond the mediocre level we were taught here. The wardens never wanted us to learn more than needed since we were supposed to be part of the mortal world.

The mortal world.

After ten years, it still feels odd to not be quite human anymore. I had human parents, lived in a human village, before I was…changed. Now I'm just a shadowborn, and I must go to this academy to learn the tricks of the trade. Part of me should at least feel excited, but I'm not. I'm more terrified than anything else. The last time I entered the Enchanted Forest, my whole world was taken from me.

"Very well, then," Maddox starts, gesturing to my trunk. "Your luggage should arrive at the academy by the time you arrive. Why don't you go stand outside with the others?"

She leaves without waiting for a reply.

I look out the window above what used to be my rickety bed. Sage is sitting on her tire swing in the back garden, looking down at Little Nessa's grave. She was a kid who used to stay here before she lost control of her power. Sage and I shared a room with her, and we always managed to calm her down when she had nightmares. But that night we went out for a fly, and when we came back, they were carrying Nessa's small body out. I remember looking at her and thinking how peaceful she looked, as if she were just sleeping. But that's the thing with shadowborns. Our magic feeds off the darkness residing within us, and often it takes over.

Our fears, our heartaches, our pain... anything that affects us negatively, the magic pulsing through our veins latches on to them and grows stronger with every fruitless effort we make to fight them.

Some of us learn to control our dark sides, at least for a while. Others, like Nessa, never stand a chance from the moment they were turned into a shadowborn. This is why the academy exists: to teach magics like me how to accept our demons instead of hiding from them. Running, avoiding, suppressing, all these things merely worsen our condition. I learned that a long time ago, and I managed to accept my demons.

The darkest one of all is named Pitch, and he's also my shadow.

Speaking of the devil, which he might be for all I know, Pitch doesn't always talk to me. I guess he doesn't really need to. His thoughts are my fears and my fears are his thoughts now. No matter where he goes, I can always sense him without looking. It's inherent, not because I want it to be, but because we're soul mates.

Literally.

The night that I died, I was the only light left within his swirling darkness, and he latched on to me by tethering my soul to his so we could both stay alive. He never meant for either of us to suffer and die. Only a child himself, he merely wanted to grant my birthday wish.

I never quite bought that either in the beginning. But despite all the anger and pain I felt towards him for many years later, I've come to accept that without him, without his darkness nestled around my heart, my soul would be incomplete. He's a part of me whether I want him to be or not, and any time we're apart, a gut-wrenching longing takes over me, and it burns right through to my core.

I turn back, seeing a shadow of a figure in the corner of the room, sitting on an empty bed. Sometimes Pitch looks like a man with broad shoulders, thick black hair, and alluring amber eyes. And sometimes, like this, he is just a shadow that blinks away before I can ask why he's even here.

Clearing my throat, I leave and head down the corridor, my navy boots announcing every footstep in the dark, dimly lit hallway. Pushing the door open, I step out into the moonlight as Sage stands and turns to me, clutching her copy of the *Book of Zorya* in her hands. This is how I know she's excited to go to the academy—she's forever reading that damn book.

"Is it time?" she asks, and I simply nod. Hooking her arm in mine, we leave the garden and head to the front of the house. We walk outside, sitting on the brick wall, watching the stars in the sky.

"They say it's so dark in the enchanted forest, and unless you have the blessing of the sun and moon, you can't see where you walk," she half-jokes, but I can tell she is nervous.

I roll my eyes at her. It can't be that bad. "You need to stop reading that book. Wait and see. We will be there soon."

She opens her book and starts reading, ignoring me completely.

"In the beginning, Aphrodite and Persephone decided to create a magical forest for all manner of creatures. They appeared in their natural form, unearthly beautiful and fae-like, and brought with them their favourite stars—the Morning Star and the Evening Star. They each placed them in the sky, and one became the sun and the other the moon," she reads out, her voice being carried by the wind to poor unsuspecting humans who don't want to hear a fairy tale like this.

A fairytale that quickly became a nightmare.

"I know, I know. Then monsters came to the forest. Blah, blah, blah," I drone but she ignores me once more and carries on reading.

"Aphrodite became known as Danica, Goddess of the Sun, and she created the Throne of Helios where she would reign over her part of the forest. Persephone became Selena, Goddess of the Moon, and she created the Throne of Luna, again where she would rule her half of the forest. To their kingdoms, they became known as the Zorya Sisters..." She stops, turning the page and pausing in whatever she's reading.

"I've heard the thrones are cursed and that's why all the royal fae are crackers," I whisper to her. Keeper Maddox and every keeper I've met talk like fae are these holy creatures and to speak badly about them is as forbidden as murder.

"Rumours, all rumours, Corvina," she sighs, snapping the book shut. "Aren't you excited to see a fae student? They're meant to be very alluring and beautiful."

Alluring and beautiful is exactly how I would describe Pitch.

But often those things just hide a person's true nature like a cloud of smoke.

When I finally focus on Sage, her all too knowing eyes are watching me closely. "I know you're scared. It's okay to admit it to me, Corvina."

"Since I became a shadowborn, I've been scared,

Sage, but I've learnt that running from it only gives the fear more power. It's better to face the darkness than run from it because one thing is for damn sure..." I pause as I see something coming down the road. "In our world, the darkness never lets you go."

Buy Here